# DREAM
## OF THE
# TRENCHES

# DREAM
## OF THE
# TRENCHES

## KATE
## COLBY

Published By Noemi Press, Inc. A Nonprofit Literary Organization.
www.noemipress.org

Cover and Book Design by Steve Halle
"Northern basket star, Gorgonocephalus arcticus, off Cape St Francis,
Newfoundland, Canada" by Derek Keats is licensed under CC BY 2.0.

ISBN 978-1-934819-80-7

How can I go on, who have just stepped over such a bottomless skylight in the bog of my life.

—Henry David Thoreau,
*A Week on the Concord and Merrimack Rivers*

# CONTENTS

*DREAM OF THE TRENCHES*

## DRIVING TO MARGARET'S MOTHER'S MEMORIAL SERVICE

In the car. Alone. A broken radio.

I-195 tracks the jagged coastline to the Cape. If I could tug every harbor and inlet taut, what would that do to distance? And if I included the space in rocks' pits and the clefts between grains of sand at the water's edge? How long would the coastline be then? I'm not sure what it is I'm wondering, exactly, without the cartographic terms to apply to it. It's something about the shortest distance between two points and the longest that's a stop on the organ of my consciousness.

Is this the difference of (not between) length and distance?

What I think is a system of units.

The acuteness and chronicity of my need and dependable inability to make sufficient distinctions keeps me afloat and adrift. The endless involution of everything and each thing keeps my eye to the pits of the grindstone while the capacity of two times the size of my metonymic heart walks around outside my chest. I can't tell the sequestering effects of fatigue from those of motherhood. The line between them and between all barely- and in-distinguishable things is where everything meets, stops, and makes further depth impossible—the vanishing line of my ability to say everything or anything at all.

If I could see the future would I have had two children, meted myself into piles of cubes of finger foods, time-outs, and time in solitary with myself on both sides of a two-way mirror? I'm sure I wouldn't not have done it, which is different from saying I'm glad I did it, which isn't not true, but "glad" reminds me of garbage and the zip-top baggies in which I pack Cheerios for the pool.

I can't see the future, but find it just as hard to pin down the conditions of the present. Is it more accurate to say that I pretty much hate the whole business but that it's full of lovely moments, or that the whole package is lovely, but made up of dreadful little eternities that gather in the cushions and crunch to dust underfoot? A perfect container makes sense of its contents. If I could swaddle the kids in snug muslin words, I'd tuck them into my elbows and return us to agreed-upon time's perennial false spring.

Along the highway green walls of creeper draw in like a hall of the backs of mirrors.

I've been thinking about agreed-upon time and rules of narrative ever since reading Ben Lerner's *Leaving the Atocha Station*. There's a contrast between the book's relatively conventional trajectory and its content, which concerns the chimerical qualities of autobiography, the insufficiencies of language that account for them, and the prohibitive temporal and organizational rules of telling anybody, even oneself, about anything.

The only hole in the story's container is that the narrator, Adam Gordon, is never taken to task for abuse of his parents' credit card. Tension escalates throughout his spending spree, and the question of how his parents and attendant load-bearing elements of the world are going to react is the lead-up to what should be the climactic comeuppance of the book.

A precept of novel-writing is that actions have consequences, known or not, but they don't just result in nothing, and there's a manifest absence at the heart of this narrative. What I want to believe happened is that Lerner wrote and then cut this conversation between Adam and his parents. He didn't know how to fix the boring scene, so he took it out and left the hole for the reader to fall into. Or walk around—often a narrative abyss is a prescription for a disjunctive way of reading, but in this case I just bypassed and understood it as lazy. Or not lazy, but that the author was so tired of trying to make it all fit together.

A laid abyss is lazy. An abyss born of exhaustion is the truest thing there is.

From the bridge spanning the longest finger of Narragansett Bay, inert brick smoke stacks bristle on the skyline's back. *Welcome to Spindle City.* A few years ago I applied for a grant to write a book of poetry interweaving the histories of Easter Island and Fall River, Massachusetts. It was going to investigate how economically insular places' successive populations lay claims to the land, displace one another, exhaust resources, and build monuments to be interpreted by future generations.

Fall River's hollow textile mills are now upstaged by a pair of monolithic cooling towers built two years ago because hot runoff from the electrical plant was killing the fish. Once, when my son was two and we were trying to sidetrack him from a tantrum, I asked, "Hey, what's that coming out of those towers, Willie?" He said, "hot dogs." When we drive by we now see all kinds of things coming from the towers—pizza, sneakers, donkeys, music.

Language is insufficient to describe the world because it seams what is made of sutures. (The correct answer was "steam.")

FEELING DESPERATE? CALL THE SAMARITANS.

I didn't get the grant to buy time from the children, to close and defend my borders, the thought of which brings a warm lump of panic to my throat that is only eased by my option of turning into the guardrail.

Sloppy raindrops begin to fall as though tossed from the sky's windows. In the uncertain edge of a summer downpour you can practically see the gravity. Steam rises.

I hadn't driven a car for more than a decade when I moved from a large city to a small one and had to concede to this cooperative form of agency in getting around. It's now one of my only available sources of relative freedom. Driving in the rain doesn't so much make me nervous as it requires that I be what I'm doing with this capsule in a bumping sea of others rather than the meniscus of and around myself I've come to love the act of driving for.

Lizzie Borden lived in Fall River. I haven't yet fit this fact into my slurry of assimilated interests, but I love questions whose answers are lost to history, of which the uncertainty of Borden's guilt is one. Are there mysteries to which there *are* no answers and never were? If I could land on one of those I'd be golden, the receding light in my rear-view mirror.

Darcie and Kate, who are the first to read everything I write, say I have no business throwing around conundrums of theoretical physics. Still, I do it all the time. I absolutely don't understand them, but their abstract mysteries are useful for things I'm trying to unfigure. For instance, I read that the fact of darkness means the universe must be contained, or:

Everything is unique.
Every thing is unique.

See?

Nothing is what it seams.

The smell of rain on hot pavement connects this moment to so many others, none of which I can remember.

Is every moment more a sequel of or serial with the one before?

A conundrum's a semantic impasse, not an actual condition of the world.

*Leaving the Atocha Station* made me uneasy in a pleasant way that is less like a roller coaster than a diagnosis. Sometimes dangerous things feel safe because you only have to survive them.

I went through a period in my twenties when I was unemployed and spent the better part of every day watching reruns of the early-90s TV series *Northern Exposure*. By late afternoon I felt softly cocooned by my existence and the permission I'd given myself to do nothing but maintain it. I am always troubled by my memory of this time when I hear the bonhomous voice of John Corbett, who either does voiceovers for numerous corporate brands or has set the standard for what the cocoon of consumerism should sound like.

A boy cups the wind with his hand out the window.

(Later I was a curator in San Francisco and miserable.)

Gift of the artist: Hold your whole life to leave it.

This is a stretch of the Interstate System.

## DRIVING TO MARGARET'S MOTHER'S MEMORIAL SERVICE

Writers tend to be preoccupied with what makes every thing unique, but I get hung up on the countless ways they clump. Moments bound by the smell of rain on hot pavement and those during which it falls on grass. Or spats against glass. Every thought I've ever had while watching a drop gather its way down the window. If I could access them all—assess a given thing within every one of its frames—maybe I could see around the edge of the meniscus or at least ease up on my tyranny over table manners.

I only met Margaret's mother a handful of times. She was a grand dame of Falmouth, renowned party-goer, supporter of causes. A sort of person with which I'm deeply familiar and that makes me think about the agreed-upon shape of time and the kinds of things one is supposed to want to do with it. I recently read Nancy Milford's 1970 biography of Zelda Fitzgerald, whose madness evidently made her refuse to wear makeup in middle age. As my grandmother would have said, she let herself go. It's hard to stay in shape. (She always made me tiptoe around the rising soufflé.)

The midpoint of my life will be the midpoint of time one day. Is it ahead of or behind me?

(Ad in the dermatologists' office: *Inject this to remove your parentheses.*)

The sun glints on hanks of wet weeds in the median. My grandmother used to cut Queen Anne's lace for the dining room on the Cape. Its florets fell into the food and all over the table like drifts of anachronistic summer snow.

## DRIVING TO MARGARET'S MOTHER'S MEMORIAL SERVICE

The word "consumed" can be active or passive to the extreme, meaning utterly actualized with attention or all used up—usefulness cancelled by use. To die of usefulness makes you a martyr, unless you die in the natural service of motherhood, say running into a house that's consumed by flames to save your own children. You consume a sandwich or take part in an economic plexus that is much bigger than you and your perceived choices, making this kind of consumption a global-capitalist misnomer that encompasses the market's fundamental mode of misrepresenting agency. (Your parents' plastic is perfect—everyone's to blame and beholden.)

You can also die, Ouroboros-style, of a kind of consumption inflicted by your body itself.

I spend so much time trying to determine when I am more or less present and whether self-actualization has more to do with the body or head or the threads between them. When I'm utterly caught up with the kids, sweating and frustrated and consumed with the putting-on of shoes, am I present or absent? Am I more myself when I am being or thinking about myself?

> Is one chronic and the other acute,
> how many points make up a line,
> great questions of our time.

What consumes me: this, my children,
my own tail. Oops. The strangest of loupes.

My sleepless nights in the visor mirror give me a little *duende* under the eyes.

When I do manage to think, I sometimes get sidetracked trying to determine if my thoughts sound like me—whether I think in the sound of my voice, I mean. And when you start thinking about your own thoughts your head collapses like a disturbed soufflé. It's then you need to look away, out where you're driving.

The car ahead says WASH ME in the same grit, stardust, and exhaust of which it is written.

The details of Zelda's illness are spotty and unspecific, so Nancy Milford just keeps reminding us she's sick by saying so. We are to agree to believe her, which is, of course, the cornerstone of authority. Zelda's only chronic symptom is her recurrent institutionalization. Toward the end she gets religious.

[(A cornerstone is symbolic. A cornice is compositional. One is a point and the other a line—a horn and a crown, respectively, etymologically. They are not related, except in relation to architecture, where neither is primarily structural.) (The Latin root of "author" is *auctor* by way of the Middle English *autor*, which is not related to the English prefix "auto-," which comes from Greek.)]

Can we agree a fake false cognate is interesting?

I don't know if the medical detail is scarce because there wasn't much available to the author or if it's another potential act of discretion and a reminder of the degree to which biography can be dated. I mean not only that the narrative modes and clichés of characterization are dated, but also that time itself can be dated— old time was a line. New time is contained in a pressured capsule hurtling at the starfield of your face. The difference is in the distance between remembering everything and having it memorized.

Between all ways and always. Between yourself and your image playing chicken in the mirror.

If your impulse is to drive a point to its limit, then you'd better go with poetry and hope to God no one notices. Or let them think what you're doing is exactly what you're doing and everyone will be none the wiser.

(The difference between "all out" and "all in" is the same.)

"Zelda Fitzgerald" is a set of qualities we've agreed on, largely thanks to the influence of this book. This is an obvious statement, but also a reminder that some things aren't real and it's hard to say when—say, autofiction or old factories upcycled as Laser Tag arenas.

SPACE AVAILABLE
WILL BUILD TO SUIT

Steeples stick from the chin of the city.

Or: everything is real and how to depict it.

Take a stack of head shots, no, screen shots—*The Autobiography of Alice B. Toklas* by Gertrude Stein plus *What is Remembered* by Alice B. Toklas plus *Tender Buttons* turns out a trembling soufflé that's real and dimensional if not known for its digestive properties.

I get dejected by the question of how to write after Stein, Woolf, Ben Lerner. What they might have in common that makes me feel flat by comparison is their ability to convey qualities of real time in words. Stein compresses subjectivity into an instant, turning a glance into a cross section of consciousness. Woolf stretches time out to a degree where either very little happens or a staggering amount of information flickers in it, depending on your perspective.

By contrast, James Joyce over-articulates, sacrificing realistic texture, the mind's deft slides and elisions. (In San Francisco's Mission District there is or used to be a donut shop with a neon sign on the fritz, blinking spasmodically in the night. I called it "the frenetic donut.") James Joyce is a frenetic donut. Jack Kerouac is one of those water snake toys from the '80s that falls out of your hand and ends up covered with lint and dog hair.

Either you want to say something or say how you say it. The latter's a form of saying itself.

No things aren't real and the image is only incidental to the mirror. And what if the mirrors are only car windows or contained in sun visors or even closer than they appear?

The mirrors, the hall of mirrors…this tired-and-true trope that Lerner and I both use because a thing is only useful if you use it. It reflects my exhaustion. If I could use it to death, smash it with my head, would a more faithful abyss open up in its stead?

Some things are only useful when pressed, even broken, and something either else or fundamental sploozes out.

> If you look closely you can see
> citrine bottles of trucker pee
> jettisoned in the median weeds.

(The difference between "reflective" and "faithful" goes both ways.)

*Leaving the Atocha Station* enacts depression and its exposure of naked time. My own experience of depression is that everything you encounter under its influence has equal weight and seems to be happening both at the other end of the tunnel and rushing at your face. Sometimes it feels like an acutely dull taste of real time relieved of words' posts and beams—time let go and oblivious to dog hair.

The writers that haunt me remove the agreed-upon relativity of things' importance and let everything fall together like a deboned duck. They foreground the sense that time is just stories in stories, receding, continuous and contained; your head a hall of literally fucking mirrors.

## DRIVING TO MARGARET'S MOTHER'S MEMORIAL SERVICE

I found someone's to-do list on the sidewalk while walking the dog this morning. Although I'll never know her, it exposed its owner like the inside of her eyelid.

Taped to the bathroom mirror:

Things to Stop Using in My Poems

mirrors (halls of mirrors, two- or three-way, etc.)
self-self-reflexivity
mise en abyme
combinatorics
recursion
involution
Ouroboros
recapitulation (ontogeny, phylogeny, etc.)
anything suggested by Hofstadter*
*modulating musical canons
millefeuille
matryoshka
loops (feedback, strange, etc.)
sets within sets of themselves

(I already *Control-F* my manuscripts for the phrase "I don't know" but let most of them stay, anyway.)

I just want you to know that I know.

I only learned there was a word for my preoccupation long after it began. I was disappointed and a little ashamed until I started to read "droste" as a portmanteau of "droll" and "triste."

Woolf and Stein each work at conveying *a* way that time can be and say something together, as bookends to a complex understanding of time. I rarely think of one without the other, which seems often to be the case for writers and especially writers who are also women. At least that seems to be the case for Darcie and Kate, who also keep writing about them in the same breath. Maybe it's that Woolf and Stein both circumvent words—the annihilating words for particular things they are trying to mean. They write around them and leave their shapes like chalk outlines at a lexical crime scene.

In Darcie's play-within-a-play she several times refers to "the poster advertising the play" and I kept crossing it out and writing in "playbill." I don't know if she hadn't thought of the word "playbill" or was purposely not using it in order to avoid the obviating properties of the exact word for the thing. I was wondering this *while* I was writing in "playbill" and thinking both that when there are words for specific things it's a shame not to use them and that calling it a "poster advertising the play" made me actually picture the thing she was referring to, while "playbill" just swallowed it.

Some noteworthy words have all but supplanted their meanings, like "antidisestablishmentarianism" and "syzygy" and "Llanfairpwllgwyngyllgogerychwyrndrobwllllantysiliogogogoch."

Also, anything onomatopoeic or palindromic and "boobless" as written in upside-down digits. Even ideograms, Imagist poems and descriptive compound nouns turn into themselves. Is the German *oberlippenbart*—"upper lip beard"—more evocative than "moustache"? "Moustache" makes me think of a picture of a Victorian man riding a bicycle with a big front wheel in my dentist's reception area. I'm sure there's a word for that.

If you could break a word into all of its associative trajectories, like a rhizomic family tree branching and rooting and intertwining with your own vast system of synapses, you'd have countless combinatoric piles of leaves—sawtoothed, silver-backed, a *millefeuille* of mirrors.

People like to say they devour or digest their art and information, but I try to go at it headlong, as through a starfield. Or I fold it into my face like an unassimilable stick of Juicy Fruit.

Not long ago I read *Madame Bovary* for the first time in maybe ten years. Both this and the last time I read it the image that stuck with me was of Emma's bedroom—the one she slowly and revoltingly expires in. Flaubert doesn't furnish much detail on the room, but I pictured it fully and specifically and completely differently each time. And my second vision of the bedroom didn't supplant the first. I can see them equally clearly and except for a lot of rough, dark wood, the rooms and the beds in which Emma dies have little in common.

What made my second vision of Emma's room so different? And why didn't it overwrite the first one? My perspectival relationship to Emma's death must have changed. It's like how even if I've labored over an email message and read it many times in draft, right after I send it I often go into my "Sent Messages" folder and read the "Sent" version as though it might give me a clue to its potential reception.

Memory is its own antimatter—the only way to keep your memories intact is to not remember them, which is why I have a desperate sense of wanting to keep the babysitter safe. She's a container of perfect memories mostly inconsequential to her and to which I thankfully don't have access.

*Leaving the Atocha Station* is a meta-book-review—an enactment, really—of the *Selected Poems of John Ashbery*. It's the kind of conceit that you typically want to disappear into the writing itself, but Ben Lerner leaves its posts and beams exposed, even the rule-of-thumb analysis of Ashbery's fake-out parataxis and free-floating pronouns.

I've been thinking about Ashbery's *you* and *we* and the way they function simultaneously as love objects and love subjects and suggested complicities of the reader, or else or maybe also they are ciphers that serve to intensify the subjectivity of the speaker. (This has been written many times before, I'm sure. I worry everything I write has been previously written and also that many of us are now trying to write like John Ashbery and hoping to God no one will notice, most of all ourselves.)

You can't say you can't say it that way any more anymore.
                                        —*Self-Portrait in a Meniscus*

In his doggedly indifferent way, Lerner's protagonist pursues a language that enacts the experience it describes. We've been doing this for a century, though, so I have a question: how many layers of meta can you effect before you come to this

                                        this

                                          this
                                          this

and so forth?

This would be to vivisect language—to break it, like a kid breaks a
radio because he wants to see how it works. But it's hard to put it
back together, to stay in shape. Your head bends out.

A: The search for meaning is the meaning.

Ah.

We are not quite ready for ourselves.

There's a difference between "occupy" and "preoccupy" but I can't figure out why. Or I can't figure out the function of the "pre-." When occupied, you are taken up with something to the exclusion of other things. What's there to be done beforehand? The "pre-" actually seems to indicate "more" rather than "before," rendering you occupied to the point of possession. Same goes for "prepossession."

(Acuteness and chronicity are different in kind.)

Q: How complicit are you in your obsessions and what do they do in time?

(A suture saves nine.)

> Etymology is pen knives
> in lovers' pockets, weeping
> sap.

Before the radio broke, I was flipping stations and caught the end of Nirvana's *All Apologies*, which I'd been mishearing for twenty years as "all in all is all we are". When I got home I finally looked up the lyrics and discovered that they were, in fact, exactly what I was hearing, redoubling my *drostesse*.

> Hold my love tonight,
> run your fingers down its spine—

I'll be in the other bed
staring into the ceiling
crack of incommensurateness.

There is something, too, in the difference between "double" and
"redouble" that feels, how do you say, chronic.

## DRIVING TO MARGARET'S MOTHER'S MEMORIAL SERVICE

There is no such thing as a cipher.

> Everything isn't real
> and nothing is certain
> but death and reflections—
>
> matryoshka made of mirrors for their faces
>
> media bleeding implements; trees, knives.

What if experience enacts the language with which it's described? We've been undoing this one for decades. But can you have it both ways, in a loop, a book review of the book you're writing and reading it—

> until it's right for now
> I have to keep at this
>
> meta-meta-onomato-
> poeia
> > *ping*

If my eyes invent what words contain for me to see, do I sleep more vividly in my dreams?

(Kate is my actual friend with whom I share a name.)

Now I lay me down to seem in the uncanny valley of autobiography.

Physically, I contain atoms and the space of their configurations.

Experientially, I only lay claim to what I know I know.

> Write to the pore, down
> to the bone, if my bones
> were made of the rest of me
> and that of everything else.

If language is inadequate to describe experience, and/or experience is shaped by our ability to describe it, does experience ever fail to live up to the scope of language? Jay Gatsby was looking for "something commensurate to his capacity for wonder." How did he know what his capacity was?

Words fail in the face of the sublime, but failure only exists in relation to success, so the sublime is still defined by the capabilities of language and located outside of its outer edge of effectiveness. So, where is the edge? What is language's capacity and what if and when do you fail to fill it? Maybe that is what "this" is—life as pure deictic—squinting into the schism, basking in the sublimity of what you could have to say if only it were real.

E. M. Forster is famous for locating language's rim—Lucy's bloody postcards, Adela's caves:

"Philip looked away, as he sometimes looked away from the great pictures where visible forms suddenly become inadequate for the things they have shown to us."
—*Where Angels Fear to Tread*

This is me in a heavy frame, eyes following my penny's fall into the fountain I wished for.

The most intriguing thing about Zelda is that it's hard to distinguish her mannerisms from her mental illness. Her biographer doesn't try. Ethically and aesthetically, this seems like the right thing to do, but it comes off as laziness or avoidance rather than suggesting our language-limited diagnostic tools' incommensurateness with human complexity. She doesn't judge Zelda, which also seems like the right thing to do, but either Zelda completely neglected and threw over her own daughter in favor of her social life and inner torment, or else Milford, with an unknown degree of purpose, made it seem that way by omission because she didn't know enough about Zelda and Scottie's relationship to depict it or perhaps lacked the capacity to imagine what might have made Zelda capable of throwing over her own daughter. Scottie is merely absent.

Did Milford do away with Scottie because she didn't fit into her narrative trajectory or did her trajectory build itself around the absence of Scottie or...something else. She doesn't speculate about Scottie. That's the right thing to do. But I can't decide whether Scottie's absence is a weak seam or needed suture. Was it laid or born of exhaustion? In either case, in being erased, Scottie remains intact, while *Zelda* only stays in shape by bulging ungainlily at the seams.

While I was reading *Zelda* I noticed a remaindered copy of Scottie's biography, written by her own daughter, on my parents' bookshelf. I haven't read it, but I guess I will, even if it's just another YOU ARE HERE on the magnifying mirror, where the pores metonymize the holes in the head.

Biography is a shoebox of agreed-upon dimensions whose breathing holes go both ways. Anyone with an eye to them knows they're a lie. Still, I prefer it to the more open mode of memoir for its allowance that darkness can be all around but not about you.

Whether short or long, time is always complete and the same shape as itself. This has something to do with distance between the self and the inside of its eyelid.

When you start habitually narrating yourself it begins to feel as though a thing hasn't happened if you can't adequately describe it. But description and narration are bound by a temporal standard that communication necessitates. So you become dependent on description for experience, and then the description compromises the experience with its falsifying strictures. Sometimes I wonder if I actually preempt some of my experiences by narrating them as or even before they happen, replacing them with their own anticipatory representations.

One meaning of "reflect" is "remember." The other is having your image cast back.

There's a note taped to my refrigerator door:

> This is just to say, suppose
> each memory is like DNA
> making sense of the whole
> if only you could decode it.

Would we not then depend upon description?

If I could, I'd tape this note to the button the door depresses to turn the light off when you close it.

Margaret is a fantastic cook, and yet the only dish she's served me that lingers in my memory was a square Pepperidge Farm layer cake from the freezer. I know it came after a very good meal only because the memory of the whole retains an aura of rarefaction. It was the kind of cake served at luncheons by upper-crust Yankee housewives circa 1983. The kind served by Margaret's mother, undoubtedly. In the kind of house containing a painting of itself.

This cake was signaling like crazy in a roomful of people, but overtaking only the two of us with its waves of hydrogenated antimatter.

—Not ironically, though. This cake was sincere as can be.

FINES DOUBLED IN CONSTRUCTION ZONE

"The sixth sense, the sense with which we read, is the ability to perceive the loss of other senses; we have lost this sense."
—Ben Lerner, *Angle of Yaw*

Some things aren't real, but agreed upon in our need for commensurateness.

The empty oculus of *Leaving the Atocha Station* is the deadly 2004 Madrid train bombings, but the only death that affects Adam Gordon is the one he invents for his mother in pursuit of sympathy from an attractive woman.

There can be no death where there isn't time and this book exists in a series of discrete instances. Adam's actions fizzle like soggy bottle rockets, with no appreciable upshots. He only reflects on his past enough to contain his continuous presence—not continuous in not resembling time, but a system of mirrors cracked like safety glass.

Typically, we try to access the abstract horror of mass tragedies through "stories"—the victims', their families', the heroes-that-rushed-into-the-flames'. It goes on for weeks in the media but here we only get one anti-story of an intellectually stymied man wrapped around a bloody catastrophe.

The term "radical subjectivity" is beyond me, but I know I'm both after and over it.

Everything isn't real, but it *is* important.

I don't know how to write anymore.

## DRIVING TO MARGARET'S MOTHER'S MEMORIAL SERVICE

Following World War II, samurai movies took off in Japan, depicting relatively useless warriors in a time of relative peace. Narratively, the films are all rising action, a ratcheting up of tension into a single climactic scene. In Masaki Kobayashi's *Samurai Rebellion*, drama builds around the fact of a stolen bride, eventually leading to a brief and thorough swordfight. The film is suffused with shadows, stiff folds of elaborate fabric, the non-rhythmic creaking and thumping of traditional instruments.

A cornerstone of samurai ethos is *seppuku*, the ritual self-disembowelment a samurai performs to either save face or avoid enemy torture. [Note the difference between "perform" and "commit" when it comes to suicide (which is more or less the opposite of that between a performance and a commitment).] *Seppuku* is weak, what a man would do, but the only suicide in this film is that of the stolen bride, who throws herself on a spear.

Following the fight scene, there is one final clash wherein the hero is forced to take down his friend with his sword, while he is himself taken down by firing of unseen gunmen. All that martial skill and intricate code of honor comes to naught, dispatched by a faceless modernity. Today we have mass shootings and large-scale acts of terror, committed in the name of God or as a performance of extreme fecklessness. The two are easily confused.

["Never" and "forever" are the same without a frame.

(Fine lines make mass graves.)]

In the end the hero dies and the dead bride's baby is taken to be raised by her wet nurse.

I've become so accustomed to the interruption of my every thought that even the most immediate, environmentally triggered—say, those I might have while walking down a leaf-strewn sidewalk in the fall—now feel distracting, as though no thought can be trusted to actually be itself. Increasingly, the only time I feel unmediated is in the act of writing, and so I've become one of those nutjobs who stops every block to press my notebook against an elm or brick wall. If I write quickly enough, it feels as though I'm snatching a thought away from evil forces of intervention. Even warm, late-morning sun through stained-glass leaves and their redolent rot feels malevolent.

> The insides of my lids
> are staticky screens
> stationary star fields
> breaking through me—
>
> a book review
> of the book you mean
> to write over.

Sometimes I worry I'm just rewriting Harry Mathews' novel *The Journalist*, in which a man becomes increasingly obsessed with indexing the entries in his diary—so much so that it consumes his life, and, therefore, itself. The book is pretty boring, but so is most conceptual writing. It's all as boring as raising children, which is what saves me—if the idea of childrearing fled and left me only with its exigencies, I might pinch out like a self-consumed star.

Is Harry Mathews still alive? Now that you can know this kind of thing just about immediately, I feel badly that I don't, as though I've neglected the idea of Harry Mathews.

Between Fall River and New Bedford a nondescript* stretch of I-195 passes through the rangy town of Dartmouth, which contains the village of Padanaram. The village was established in the nineteenth century by a prominent resident named Laban Thatcher who identified with the Biblical Laban for whom he was named, himself an inhabitant of the Mesopotamian plain of Padan-Aram.

{I don't know of a noun denoting a person after whom one is named. There is "namesake" for the person receiving the name, but none for that bestowing it. How is it possible that such a useful word does not exist?

[A word with an opposite meaning for which there is no word screams in the dark like a frenetic donut. (But are there words with no opposite meanings? The opposite of "tree" could be anything, "everything" or nothing. No—"thing.") (*"Nondescript" has no antonym in "descript," which would say and/or mean the same thing, anyway.)]

There are also words that function as their own antonyms, like "mirror-image," which suggests that two things are either the same or opposed. We are *literally* and *virtually* and their own autogamous opposites in a hall of mirrors, where we agree to disagree more often than we think.}

The Biblical Laban had many children and is a symbol of fatherhood. The Dartmouth Laban begot a hulking saltworks known as "Laban's Folly" that barely existed its way into the twentieth century. I heard the other day that they are going to shut down the ancient Fall River electrical station, even though they've just built the cooling towers.

Q: What do you call a modern-day "folly"?

A: a joke
A: a disaster
A: an ill-conceived project
A: bananas

We named Willie for my father. His name is a homonym, which is an obsolete synonym of "namesake." I learned this online, but still don't know if Harry Mathews is alive. I just want to finger my little laid abyss for a minute.

It's always disorienting to read an obituary for someone I hadn't known was still alive. I just read Doris Lessing's and realized I'd confused her winning the Pulitzer Prize a few years ago with her death.

Not long before this (which wasn't very long, at the time of writing), Darcie, Kate and I were talking about how Lessing abandoned her two young children to pursue her writing career in another country. Darcie said it's what a man would do, meaning it was weak. I have to agree. Lessing laid herself—an abyss, I mean.

{[Some organisms reproduce via autogamy, which has an antonym in "allogamy," that refers to cross-fertilization (and another seeming one in "bigamy," which is false since it applies to marriage, not reproduction, and humans can't self-fertilize), but not one for the act or process of consuming or cancelling yourself out—of unproducing yourself.] [Things can have more than one opposite, though. (Is there a word denoting "one of several opposites"? Is this one possible definition of "paradox"? I'm sure there's more than one antecedent of "this," and the macroscopic universe is only a collection of microscopic ones, after all. I read that somewhere. The degree to which they recapitulate one another might be the answer to

Q: this?)]}

My children unbirth me like a star does itself. It was an accidental unpregnancy and in trying to enact it

> I am Silly Putty
> in my own hands
> pressed into my palm
> my peeled-away
> impression.

Doris Lessing's *The Golden Notebook* interweaves excerpts of the narrator's three topically indexed journals with excerpts of a fourth containing a mise-en-abyme autobiographical novel. The last, golden, notebook brings it all together.

(*The Golden Notebook* is a work of fiction.)

Modernism pretty much did or pointed at the possibility of doing everything. You can only do more of it or fulfill its possibilities or eject it all like a sour ball from the airway of Resusci Annie.

(Q: What about John Ashbery?

A: There is no such thing as a cipher.)

Conceptual writing is a problem and the problem is its point. It's anachronism 2.0, always swallowing and unbirthing itself, its opposites and the arguments against it like a figuratively fucking autogamous water snake.

(Is "this" what's known as destabilizing authorship or its opposite?)

(Nothing isn't real. I'm tired of talking about it.)

Q: What do you call a thing that consists of the hole in its middle?

A: conceptual
A: matryoshka
A: donut

Scent of dryer sheets curls into cold, dark street. Don't look back or turn to a pillar of light.

Of course there's no word for having or being more than one op-posite—loads and the conditions under which they are borne have a limit. And given the non-existence of this and other would-be essential words, it seems a shame to not use all those that do exist.

Nevertheless, I found this list taped to my forehead. (Wisely, I wrote it in the mirror, so its mirror-image is the same as itself.)

Things Everyone Should Stop Using in Their Poems
armature
apertures
excessive use of lenses
"slippage"
most applications of water fowl*
bracken, brambles
grackles
Möbius strips (I use these all the time, but it doesn't annoy me)
"this" to mean "this"

The word that bugs me most might be "architecture." Build it or don't, but tell me how.

Structural opposites are both joined and differentiated by a key-stone, which combines the symbolic, decorative and load-bearing functions of a cornice and a cornerstone. The keystone of language is what it lacks (I mean that every / which way.) The keystone of the universe is either matter or a hole or if there's such thing, nothing. (There are probably physical things and anti- and non-things other than these, but I don't know them. Also, since the set of all sets is a member of itself, maybe there's no keystone, but a shape that slips through itself like a water snake / my ear, nose and throat choked with dog hair.)

Even if the universe is not structurally sound in that it's likely to either disintegrate or collapse, it appears to distribute its weight evenly, just as "donut hole" denotes both the gap at the center of a pastry or a spherical pastry around which there is nothing. "Donut hole" is its own antonym. "Donut" is not, though, which seems uneven (*unless there's a German word for "turducken").

Is the opposite of "donut" its actual hole, a spherical pastry, a caraway scone, or the scent of bruised moss as experienced by a mole in the wake of a galloping cavalcade at the edge of a medieval glen?

A: All of the above. Also *millefeuille*.

Words are boards to a broken window. To keep the specters in.

When I was in graduate school for writing I was frequently assigned to try to write in someone else's style. This practice of emulation was supposed to instill flexibility and break bad habits (my excessive use of "this," for instance). My first book contains the results of an exercise in writing like Gertrude Stein. But once you start writing like Stein, in particular, it's very hard to stop, and then you have another habit to break. Years later, I'm scared of unwanted influence and sometimes avoid or delay reading things I fear will steer me, or worse, that will turn out to be better incarnations of the thing I'm at present trying to write.

I became a poet when I fell in love with one in my early twenties and began imitating his writing in an effort to woo him, which I for the most part failed to do. I kept writing anyway, but the habit of imitating him was hard to kick. And in spite of how palpable the aura of my former preoccupation with this poet still is, I can hardly recall any details of our actual relationship. There was a party at which the poet played "Piano Man" on the piano. (Oddly, twenty-odd years later I would write a poem about "Piano Man" for a different poet I was in love with at the time of its writing.)

The OuLiPo had a term, "plagiarism by anticipation," that I want to apply to *Leaving the Atocha Station*, although it might more aptly be applied to Lyn Hejinian's *My Life*, which I've long had a sense I should have written, in that it's diectic.

An oculus is the opposite of an aperture whether, thus, or because full of sun.

(Please don't make me look up.)

I am going to write the opposite of a roman à clef, with real names but where everyone's a fake or a cipher*—

a Cubist portrait of the artist in the postmodern mode. Cubism gone wild. Cubism in the fourth dimension, as sixthth sense, in syzygy with itself.

It's called *Dream of the Trenches.*

Doris Lessing got me thinking about how newspapers write obituaries for famous people in anticipation of their deaths—elderly heads of state, reckless teen actresses. (Harry Mathews...?) It was only about a week after Nelson Mandela died that I started seeing ads for his big-screen biopic. Conversely, I've heard about the release of movies made on topics not-yet-sensitive at the time of making being delayed until unforeseen dust had settled. Oh, and Tom Sawyer attending his own funeral.

Do these count as incidences of anachronism? I think of this word as denoting schisms in time, but have a feeling I take liberties with it. What do you call things that preexist what they signify?

*Maybe not fakes or ciphers, but green screens behind which things happen. Names aren't that important.

I still don't know how to write anymore.

## DREAM OF THE TRENCHES

Our dark corners no longer contain us. Don't tell the children. A brightness bears down.

I tell the children how trenches knuckle down from the ocean floor, dark water the opposite of mountains. Inside, kissing the earth's core, hydrothermal vents host colonies of creatures.

Suppose the sun died and all life on the earth's surface with it. Orange tube worms and white crabs would still wave and scud in hot currents underneath the black frozen sea.

We were in a field. Our children ran ahead, laughing, whacking tall weeds at the perimeter with sticks. Fescue and sharp thistle. Soft green timothy.

We begin to fade in the bright, thick heat. Above and all around us, two-way holes are healing.

The highway divides New Bedford's patchwork of shuttered brick factories, endangered fish-packing plants and family law offices housed in former chandlers' shops. The city doesn't feel layered so much as half-folded into itself like temporal marble cake.

If I had forever and an endless involuting writing surface, I'd diagram my memory—what gets privileged, how does it affect what else I remember, what else I do. Memory's trawled net and its slippery contents *make* time, though—if I could chart memory's tangled ecology, forever's how long it would make.

Several times a summer we take the ferry from New Bedford to Martha's Vineyard to visit my in-laws. The trip only takes an hour, but with the kids insensible to the vulnerability of their teeth, climbing over the seats, reeling between steel columns, it's as long as an hour can be. In spite of how many times I've taken this trip and how many more I will take, I know that one day they'll each be overwritten by one aggregate memory of ferry-to-the-Vineyard. Unless I record or memorize them, the details will be buried deep and safe in my memorial matryoshka.

("Overwritten" and "overridden" are almost homonyms and almost synonyms. This seems like a bad seam. No. This seams like a bad seem.

{Also, these two-way words that mean both exactly what they mean and what they don't [two-way meaning directed back at itself, like a three-way mirror (a two-way mirror is really a one-way window)]—not like "one way," which is its own opposite, in that it either means "restricted" or "one of many possible ways" [e.g., "Some Trees"], but like "insensible," which means both not perceiving and imperceptible. Is this due to our lexical laziness or a depthless abyss of complexity?

["Depthless" means both "shallow" and "deep."]})

Old factories make good self-storage. If I had forever and lived in New Bedford, I'd keep myself safe, if not survivable. (I'll never survive myself.)

Driving under and over stars and between them, getting closer to some, further from others, on this hundred-mile drive to Woods Hole.

Poetry is where I recognize the sources of my torment and find new ones. Beauty and horror are flipsides of torment—a flipside not like the lesser half of a record, but the opposite of the idea of front or back—each opposed to the other, but together amounting to the thing itself.

Q: Is a flipside an opposite of "opposite"?

(Written in the margin of Draft Eight: *Make Q and A characters in a play?*)

A: There's no such thing as opposites.

Nevertheless, the cores of many prefix-dependent words reject the opposites of their prefixes, like "nevertheless" and "furthermore," which cantilever into the abyss. Furthermore, isn't "furthermore" kind of baroquely redundant? There must be a lot of dark matter to account for these imbalances.

But where is the dark matter? (This is me shining my penlight at the night.)

"Alwaystheless" and "closermore" are among the most useful non-words I can think of.

Things for which there are no words are the holes that words fall into.

What kind of sense is actually in the world and what kind do we put into it? We know what subjectivity means, but what is it to be objective? We can't perceive past the limits of our sensory equipment—nor speak of what we'd see there—so is objectivity a blind trust of vision or a consensual dissembling? (I first wrote "dissemblance," but that both is and means a different thing.)

Following a century's-worth of formal experiment in disjunction, interruption, irony and recursion—and within our current mise en scène of flat, low-grade sensation and barely distinguishable qualities of information—what is the value of depiction?

In Book Two of *My Struggle* Karl Ove Knausgaard talks about having lost his faith in literature and stories: "[T]he nucleus of all this fiction, whether true or not, was verisimilitude and the distance it held to reality was constant. In other words, it saw the same." He goes on to say that the only forms of writing he now finds value in are diaries and essays:

> ...the types of literature that did not deal with narrative, that were not about anything, but just consisted of a voice, the voice of your own personality, a life, a face, a gaze you could meet. What is a work of art if not the gaze of another person? Not directed above us, nor beneath us, but

at the same height as our own gaze. Art cannot be experienced collectively, nothing can, art is something you are alone with. You meet its gaze alone.

("Alone" means two times there.)

Memory is totally verisimilitudinous and unreliable. The truth is to make it anew anymore.

A poet's a samurai run through by his sword.

(Mine's a double-edged deictic.)

I found out Harry Mathews died in the time between writing this and publishing it.

Between New Bedford and the Cape the ice-shoved moraines of the Elizabeth Islands define the outside edge of Buzzard's Bay. The small island of Penikese lies toward the end of the chain. In the early twentieth century it housed a leper colony, the only vestige of which is a small cemetery. In the 1970s a school for troubled boys opened, with a capacity of only nine students. It closed in 2011. Both institutions were government-funded prisons.

"To meet as far this morning / From the world as agreeing / With it…"

I could spend all my time thinking about these lines. I could give myself up to them—leave my family, my comfortable life, the dog, lock myself in a cellar or aerie and spend the remainder of my inward-curling days staring at my hands or the sky and trying to understand those lines. Or make an endless list of ways to resolve them and a second endless list of impediments to resolution. Or I could write them on a million slips of paper and eat them, swallow their abyss with my being.

Among the catalog of horrors you might suffer during pregnancy, the condition called "pica"—the urge to ingest non-food items such as ash, plaster, clay, and paper—seems overrepresented in the literature. I think it's quite rare, but the idea of it is so fantastic—what if you could eat whatever you want, keep it safe by consuming and personally destroying it, like a boy breaks a toy to keep the other kids from playing with it. The world would then really be your oyster—the edible part, I mean, not the pearl, although you could eat that, too, and contain a small moon.

<u>Non-Food Items I'd Like to Eat</u>
stars, steam, holes, leaves
all my motifs
their flipsides, opposites and *faux amies*
the OED
The Collected Works of John Ashbery

How to write after John Ashbery.

At night, by the fire, we take turns telling made-up stories. And we talk of the vents. "There are eyeless shrimp, bumping in hot eddies."

Eyeless! We've heard of blind spiders that evolved in the dark of deep caves, but they have eyes, at least, even if useless. To adapt to a place with no light…the idea consoles us as the shadows curl in from the edges like *trompe l'oeil* wallpaper.

And still, in a lightless, even eyeless place, things have color—orange worms, white crabs. Black mats of limpets. The swaying arms of anemones are translucent, even lacking light to filter through them. To our faith in these traits we cling like limpets.

The fire subsides into low, quavering coals. We stroke the children's heads with our upper lips, push our noses in their hair. A sweet, overripe scent suffuses us.

Margaret went through a period of doing handstands. It seemed like an equilibrating gesture, a rough equivalent of my smoking. I was twenty-two and had no regard for my health. Margaret was twenty-four and maybe starting to feel the curvature of the meniscus.

New Bedford's sea of rusty derricks is an occupational graveyard. Not only is the ocean mostly strained of marketable fish, but its ecology has been upended by ships discharging ballast water far from home. Invasive mollusks and mitten crabs kink up the food chains. Jellyfish bloom. Memory is like this—what relocated fact or protozoan moment will decimate what would be the whales.

> *Time: I don't know*
> *Place: Glass atrium of the New Bedford Whaling Museum*
> *Characters: Yes*

Q: What is a whale?
A: Monstrous repository of mankind's torment
A: Benevolent bulb-head that bobs on children's walls
Q: Is this an actual opposite or flipside or the longest distance between two same points?
A: Nothing isn't real.
Q: All the time?

*(A loud ticking we've only just noticed but would have at-
tributed to a clock had we heard it earlier, now turns out to be
either the flipping sound of a film projector or a pink cartoon
rabbit tap dancing atop a magician's hat.)*

A: I frame my shots like a director with her hands. *(Paus-
es)* Have to squint, which is looking at the backs of
your lids.

Q: Don't they tremble?

A: Other times I tuck the images in with my finger, then
reach around and pull them, neatly linked, from my
fist.

*(Both look up at the sky for a moment, then at their hands, and
then A turns to leave.)*

Q: What's that all over your back?

A: Or my front.

Q: Is that dog hair?

A: Ahoy matey, I'm Möbius Dick!

*ping*

Turns out this is actually a twisted filmstrip and I am the one ad-
vancing the frame.

(Also, it's only a vehicle for the stars—I play both Q and A.)

Marion. Mattapoissett. The South Shore's mishmash of Anglo and Indian names meets at Mashpee and the association with mashed peas it's carried for me since I was a child. In Algonquin the name means something along the lines of "great water"—"great" meaning "big." Why do we not now just say it means "big water," then?

One Christmas Eve, in the absence of a Bible, my father-in-law read the King James Christmas story to us from his phone. He'd never read it to us before, but seemed to have a sudden urge to play patriarch. He was sitting in a rocking chair by a roaring fire and everything.

Q: What do you call a two-way anachronism? I mean a closed loop of one—two anachronisms of equal weight that require one another.

A: absence
A: presence
A: syndeictic
A: dodonut

"Great" does evoke something that "big" doesn't. It suggests time and God and awe and gratitude and a manner of being that no one alive has ever witnessed. What do you call words that outlast what they signify? (This is the opposite of Tom Sawyer's funeral, which is itself the opposite of a way to postdate words, hang them like flypaper and wait to see what sticks. For instance, before she was born I planned to name the baby for my grandmother, but we didn't.)

What if words were cumulative? They could hold so much more, like, "great big water." This is not a good example, though, since "great big" is a thing that we actually say. It does contain a tinge more awe than "big," but not as much as "great."

(The mise en scène turns out to be the scenery, the back of which I burst through, screaming.)

If I had forever and could say it, that's when I'd know I'd really made it.

I've always wanted to write about Christmas. Its plastic container of kitsch and cultural nostalgia for an innocence that never existed is getting deeper by the minute. It seems to me that people have pretty suddenly stopped complaining about the creeping-up of the season. We want to feel something, all-year-round if necessary.

Christmas is a non-non-site, in the Smithson sense,[1] celebrating the would-be non-site of itself. The negatives don't cancel but make a third thing that's either both negative and positive or neither—the other opposite of a double negative. To write what I mean about it is a form of non-writing.

(Is all writing non-writing?)

(The difference between *meta-* and *non-* is either nothing or something I must think about.)

[Let's say "abyme" is a portmanteau of "abyss" and "me." (Although, in French, it just means "abyss.")]

---

[1] Which is an abstract[2] work of figurative information—a thing removed from and representing a site but not (unordered in not) resembling it?

[2] The opposite of abstraction is figuration, but "figurative" is its own opposite, meaning rendered either in likeness or metaphor.[3]

[3] I don't know how to mean any/more.

Pamela Lu's roman à clef *Pamela* came out right before 9/11 and I've since had the phrase, "We missed being real by 50 years or so" stuck in my head. And we are now even less real than that, which is yet another feather for my capsule.

Dear Future Me,

Memory is a cipher
whose key you've always already swallowed.

Memory is its own antimatter
and this distance between it's the key to what might be

the difference between a roman- and a memoir-à-clef—

—Me

Is the only difference between autofiction and roman à clef whether you've changed the names? This is a thing to ask of Darcie and Kate.

## DREAM OF THE TRENCHES

Self-sufficiency is a sieve. You drain and leave yourself behind, thinner and more concentrated each time, free of texture and indigestible bits of spice, string and gristle.

Yes, we are making it, sandbagging our extents, adapting to the dark and mistrusting any stray forms of light. At night we gasp beneath the projected stars, whose brittle sparkle seems to fill our breathing holes.

We withdraw our heads, admire our thickening chitinous parts, are so intent on our hermitic facilities that the children worry they will forget to breathe. We leave sticky notes to remind them:

Inhale, exhale,
repeat. Blink
if you can
*blink.*

## DRIVING TO MARGARET'S MOTHER'S MEMORIAL SERVICE

Yesterday at the time of writing I gave Willie a phone book and let him tear out all the pages. I was so exhausted that rather than mop the kitchen floor I started reading Draft Five and decided not to cut the following:

"Stricken out with a suture on Page 47, Draft Three: ~~Abyme me up, Scottie!~~"

I need a poultice of puncture wounds. To bleed out/through.

Look out the window. Feel thick in the heat; feedback of weather, seasons, the sound of the container you're in; the wind in the roof rack. Each frame of thought has countless ambient impetuses furnishing the tension without which your head would fall together like a deboned duck.

(By "frame" I mean as in a film strip, where a frame is its own opposite—a thing enclosing some form of content as well as framed content),

i.e., everything is unique.

Q: What is "everything"?

A: every thing
A: nothing actual or actually nothing

A: the set of all sets that's a member, etc., only actively: "to apply the same process to the process itself" [I want this to define "praxis," but it's the definition of "double thought" from *1984*. (What's the name for a fake false friend? Is it actually "friend"?)]

A: meta-reflexive hypotaxis

A: "this"

A: another damned donut hole (Q: What's the difference between a red herring and motif?)

I see municipal water towers painted with the names of their towns. Turbines. Turgid green summer leaves. The green-black undersides of overpasses.

When green is so dark it looks black, is it green or black? There's also that.

I can't quite remember, but Margaret's mother was in the social register and/or used to consult it. She had a guest book. My mother has a guest book and is a tyrant about it. She'll move it around the house so that it's always seemingly serendipitously under visitors' noses and then she'll end up having to ask them to sign it, anyway.

She once gave me a guestbook that I leave in the attic bedroom, but only about a third of our visitors sign it, which seems to render the whole thing pointless, so I understand my mother's obsessiveness. Maybe I'll throw mine away. Or tear out the blank pages and eat them, send them through the hole at my center.

(Because nothing isn't real and how I feel it.)

While some things' usefulness is cancelled by use—say, a tube of toothpaste—a name can't be used up and its usefulness is generally proportionate to the frequency of its employment. But there's a flipside in that it's possible to wear names out, render them limp, especially those that designate horrors.

Say "waterboarding" ten times fast. Say "sucking chest wound." Say "Wounded Knee."

See?

A: There's nothing to see here. Move along.

I have a flashbulb memory of coming home late one time when I was in my teens. It was December and there was snow and when I entered my cold, street-lit bedroom I saw my mother had placed a tinsel angel I'd been given as a baby on my dresser. I remember the snow and the cold and the light and the date and the glinting angel compounding into an overall sense of "Christmas" as a marker of time that brought me to tears.

A: This affective gestalt, this immanence, is the ghost machine.

Description is a water snake, made of its hole.

A star is a future hole.

Is the purpose of art to mirror or mimic the experience of being alive?

(Evidence of absence: You can't see your own eyes move in the mirror.)

In the fifteenth century painters discovered linear perspective— the more realistic rendering of objects as proportionately smaller with distance from the eye. With it, the visible world, rather than the ethereal and conjectural one, took center stage in European art. Now zoom out to the turn of the 1970s and the simultaneous rise of the seemingly opposed photorealist and conceptual art movements, both in which creation has left the premises and the empty house plays to itself. Whether the house is thereby rendered a vessel of containment or a vehicle of vehicularity and/or/if in which respective case I can't say; but in any case, the material object is replaced by mirrors and language, whose ultimate function might be the same.

Correlative *faux ami* (I know that's at least half redundant), but my birth coincided with this twin apotheosis and antithesis of representation (I'm not at all sure of the difference).

Once I read an ethics column about a woman's daughters concealing from her the fact of her impending death. To not know the answer to the question that haunts your whole life, even if you never think about it, leaves you forever incomplete.

How and when it will end?

What it all comes to: a head.

I've claimed so many arrangements of stardust and their names. My home is a cumulative tomb I fill up into. How to debone it.

> Living Room
> Upright piano—moved from childhood home in Massachusetts
> End tables—handed down from husband's parents
> Glass lamps—wedding presents
> Striped armchair—San Francisco, 2006
> Red couch—Providence, 2007

What's the operative difference between naming a thing and describing it and which comes closer to nailing it and/or the lid on its casket? Which is at what distance?

On our way from California to Rhode Island we drove through South Dakota. We left Wounded Knee late morning and got to the Badlands in the harsh light of midday, when the landscape is flat and nearly characterless. Is "Badlands" more itself at times of slanted ochre light, and to really experience it would I have to leave my car and hike out into it (how far?) and run out of water or smoke a cigarette or meditate or shout into the abyss or meniscus and for how long?

Where do the experiential capacity of Badlands and my capacity to experience it meet?

The living room also contains toys, photographs, knick knacks, old books handed down from grandparents: *The Diary of Samuel Pepys*. The couch is filthy from the children's feet, Cheerio dust, rubbed-off starscreen.

Approaching the Cape, the vegetation becomes battened-down and thrashed, the trees bent like ideas of babushkas. Even in the glutinous heat, the town of Onset makes me think of dark and winter and illness. Is there ever an onset of something you want?

The highway is lined with cranberry bogs. The bogs of Onset. For some time now this phrase has been turning in my head like a broken record. *The bogs of Onset.*

> Record player—bought online around 2009
> TV—Best Buy, 2010
> Oil-on-board still-life—Providence junk shop, 2014
> Tapa-cloth map of Tonga—Tonga, 2000
> Coffee table—handed down from parents, covered with coffee rings
> Tattered rug—handed down from Margaret, to whom it was handed by her mother

This is bananas. Stop it.

A "broken record" plays over and over while my broken radio is just broken. They are opposites and respective opposites of "dead air"—dead air as broadcast, not that breathless kind of July, both of which bristle with electricity, although whether I perceive or project that, in neither case can I tell. We are natural-born receivers of, if nothing else, ourselves.

If you were to bury yourself alive and rub your eyes, glowing green floaters would still scroll by. Staticky screens on the backs of the lids recapitulate the night sky. Meanwhile, the actual night sky is all around us, but overwritten by so much light, both artificial and its own, it can hardly be seen. This incandescent cataract is the dog hair in my ingrown eye.

I am driving in the space between all of the stars—the space that should be dark, contained, as we are, by the bogs of Onset.

## DREAM OF THE TRENCHES

There is a lot of gray area when it comes to light. Of this we warn the children. For instance, we are accustomed to calling light that is not furnished by the sun "artificial," but many life forms create their own.

In a bioluminescent sea at night, motion lingers in lambent swashes.

The green flash at sunset is attributed to a variety of phenomena, including a "mock-mirage" effect, which is so outside-in we wish we could live in it like hothouse tomatoes.

So, there is mock-mirage light, too. Whether it's fake or not we haven't figured.

But we have to distinguish the different kinds, or we might find we were mistaken about everything.

Pamela Lu captures that degree of containment by your head that makes you want to burst screaming from your eye holes. Both she and Ben Lerner talk about "experience" as though it were a dead-made thing with pinned wings to place under a cloche and look at. I want to say that Lu does this better than Lerner, but her novel has no plot. That is its point. It's a protracted scenario, a discrete and endless presence. Lerner rolls his scenario into its interior like a water snake toy—shit—no, scarf—tucked with his finger into his fist, then whipped out the other side, where the world is and things happen.

*Pamela* came out in 1998 and a lot of things have happened since then that might now make utter interiority intolerable and disingenuous. Maybe we as a culture have been whipped out the other side of our self-self-indulgence. Also, after the unspeakable horror of seeing my kid get shoved on the playground, I know I no longer live inside my eye holes.

Actually, *Pamela* knows all of this. It's semi-self-satirical and knows how exhausting and wretched it is. *Leaving the Atocha Station* is mostly earnest and also knows how exhausting and wretched it is, as well as how artificial both its earnestness and knowing wretchedness are.

I'm too tired to write about it. (Pick your abysses or blink freneti-
cally in the night.)

I wonder how Lerner and Lu write after each other.

How often do people know how they die and how often when? Which would I rather know less? What upset me most about C.D. Wrights's untimely death might be that after having written so much about dying she went suddenly in her sleep. Which is the dream.

(The woman whose daughters concealed her terminal diagnosis was losing her memory at the same time. They figured she wouldn't retain the information.)

When a person dies of old age or after a long illness, his or her life assumes an arc with a decorative keystone made of its content. When a famous person dies abruptly in his or her prime, a biographer attains the agreed-upon shape of time with a plastic protractor of foreboding.

The arc is a lid—a blinking meniscus—with static on the back.

The arc is how we can't keep our memories intact.

The arc is the interrogation light whose curvature confuses you with its recapitulation of the earth, your eyeball, the donut hole of your self-comprehension.

Zelda wrote two semi-autobiographical novels, the second left unfinished when she died in a fire. Nancy Milford devotes a lot of time to analyzing them as though they were the key to the dark matter of Zelda's existence rather than the twinkling switchboard of Zelda's wishful reading of herself (which isn't to say that those things might not be the same).

Like "boobless" written in upside-down digits, some shapes take the place of the things they once stood for. Letters and figures. Hearts and stars. Per my experience with Willie, this starts to happen around age three.

Whenever she learned of a long-suffering person's death, my grandmother would say, "Well, that's a promotion." She bequeathed me her set of Samuel Pepys {mispronounce it and it won't rhyme [related/red herring: at the time of writing, I don't know how to say "Ove," but (hope to) know by Draft Nine]}.

A cross wreathed with dead roses near Exit 25.

There are mostly words for categories of things, not for each incarnation of "leaf," for instance. (Does a unique thing have more or fewer qualities than something found in quantity?*) Description tucks its subject inside both concentric and contiguous containers, where it recedes like the innermost matryoshka between two mirrors.

(Fun fact: *Control-F* this book for "both," take that number, double and redouble it.)

(By "fun" I mean "faux," à la "fun fur.")

Language is its own anti-matter. But what if you could move faster than the tags of its self-suicidal lasers, slide right out from each and leave a sea of honest-to-goodness meanings in your wake?

To your sucking chest wound of acute wonder and chronic ineffability apply the bleeding poultice of poetry.

(Take two of "both" and two of "this" and then call me in the morning.)

Q: Which is the truer portrait: what I consume or what consumes me?

*Is this a real or fake or false or only seeming question? (Side note: I no longer know the difference between a footnote and parenthesis.)

## DRIVING TO MARGARET'S MOTHER'S MEMORIAL SERVICE

Mirages on a hot highway look more like water than that alongside which I'm driving. It's weird that water is the very thing you're most likely to need in the conditions producing the illusion of it—à la a *Loony Toons* desert oasis. Before the radio broke, it once occurred to me how many dance songs there are about dancing—and love songs about love—that popular music is often about the feeling it's intended to induce, having chewed the feelings for you. A love poem, on the other hand, might just as easily be about composting as it is about love. A love song is unlikely to concern composting, though, and a dance song? Forget it.

["Mirage" is neither related to "mirror" nor "peerage," with which it seems like it should rhyme, and which has nothing to do with "peering," as into a mirror. (A peerage is a social register.) ("Pepys" is pronounced "peeps.")]

If I could only stop writing this…I'm so tired of trying to make it fit together.

(Someone had blundered.)

*1. Please continue.*

Epitaph by anticipation: an Applebees billboard in the voice of John Corbett.

## DRIVING TO MARGARET'S MOTHER'S MEMORIAL SERVICE

Let's say there's a line between fidelity and readability and then wonder how close you can get to it before tipping into *this*-ness. And how you stand to remain on this side.

Is this the butt-end of literature, where feckless speakers talk about what they're doing and failing to do at the same time they're doing and failing to do it? Is this all that's left? Your nose pressed up to your head in a cloche?

[I mean a bell jar, not the hat, like those which Zelda wore. (I am not here / to speak of Plath.)]

Like *Leaving the Atocha Station*, Juliana Spahr's and David Buuck's *An Army of Lovers* is about how poetry has lost its *raisons d'être*— that it's now naïve to credit poetry with political power, even though poets like to believe that all speech acts are political, so what's left is to talk about the schism and to call our talk of it the act of creation and the created thing together. It's about the search for a way to make poetry do something while trying to make it be something, and failing at both. That built-in claim of failure gives the project a watertight argument against itself, making the argument for the book the same as the argument against it. It's quite brilliant, really. It's conceptual.

The characters can't actually make or write anything because they seem to find all deliberate manifestations of form artificial, cute, and thus want to create—no—*be* pure content.

I was not asked to furnish one, but here's a blurb for *An Army of Lovers*:

> What you think I'm doing is exactly what I'm doing and I need you to know that I'm smarter than that. I'm smarter than you.
>
> —*An Army of Lovers*

And yet, this book is terrified of being and being thought clever. The speakers call themselves "mediocre poets," but what they mean is that "poetry" is the closest available word for what they do, the latter being something quite above and beyond and also deliberately beneath "poetry"—"poetry" cannot accommodate them. They are not mediocre at "poetry;" "poetry" is mediocre at them. Their self-reflexive, -suicidal, meta-political mise-en-abyme performance of themselves and everything reflected behind them in the mirror is a failure that enacts failure, and so I have to admire how close this book is to being itself. I threw it at the wall around page 31, where there appears a rhapsodic, cata-logic, pseudo-populist, post-Whitmanian vision of all late-cap-italism's meta-inauthentic products and defenses shimmying si-multaneously in a spectacle with a budget exactly that of the US government.

Picture a panopticon where you're both at the center and at every point of its circumference. Also, you both helped to build and are chipping away at the facility with your flimsy plastic spoon. Each night you are served the full life story of your last meal, which changes every day, but is only ever always the same thing as it is and always was.

Whenever I try to plan my last meal, a tender filet is overwritten by institutional crinkle-cut fries on a sick-green plastic plate.

All conclusions are drawn. How about French theory vs. French fries and how much of each you ate.

## DRIVING TO MARGARET'S MOTHER'S MEMORIAL SERVICE

Around Draft Four, Kate tells me that "penny farthing" is the term for a Victorian bicycle with a big front wheel. Darcie says there's also a word for the smell of rain on hot pavement. She might mean "petrichor," which I didn't know of before searching for it, but which specifically refers to the smell of rain on dry earth.

I am showing you my work, the praxis and the process, in service of the truth. But the reality is the scenery—the barriers and bogs—will turn out to be the epilogue.

In the margin of Draft Seven I scrawl: *starfield / of hot dogs.*

I'm preoccupied with stories of artists dying in the service, or the actual making, of their art—Robert Smithson's plane crash while surveying a site for an earthwork, Eva Hesse's fume-induced brain tumor. It's already my privilege to die while writing, if as yet not of it.* It's a truism that truth is found in fewest words, which my life-shaped logorrhea either verifies or disproves.

Elena Ferrante once said in an interview, "…writing, for me, is above all a battle to avoid lying. If it seems to me not that I've won but that I've fought with all my strength, I decide to publish." Without understanding either the nature of the truth or the tenor of my lies, that feels right.

With the credit card and the train bombing, Lerner twice omits the sword fight.

Autofiction is *seppuku*, both performed and committed in the service of the real.

Q: What's the difference between reality and truth?

*2. The experiment requires that you continue.*

Perhaps the nostalgia of Christmas isn't for a non-existent time of innocence, but for a time when we believed such a time existed.

"God" is names for light.

*I am still alive at the time of writing.

## DRIVING TO MARGARET'S MOTHER'S MEMORIAL SERVICE

After graduate school I found a job as a copywriter at a gift cat-alog. I would be briefed on a product's features and then write a "story" to sell it—something to imbue a set of grilling tools, say, with a seeming long history. I quickly learned that almost any con-sumerist frippery—lockets, cufflinks, "heirloom" baby gifts—can in some way be attributed to the Victorians, who were, after all, the inventors of pre-chewed sentiment. At the same time as each product had its own story to tell, it would allow the gift recipi-ent to tell *their* story, creating a beautiful figure-eight of narrative significance for a piece of laminate junk mass-manufactured with cheap labor on the other side of the world.

This storytelling imperative has become a cliché in advertising. From cars to bath products to the credit cards you buy them with, a wide range of consumer products now claims that it will help you to tell and/or become a part of your unique story. (While "unique" used to mean the opposite of "nondescript," it now most often means "nondescript," so which is its true or actual mean-ing?) One way that retail companies I've since written for promote this "story" business is with personalization, e.g., monograms and birthstones. (It was the Victorians who popularized birthstones and ascribed their months and meanings.)

If you search "history of birthstones," "birthstone chart" or "birthstone origins" on the internet you will find countless versions of the same story and the same chart with the same supposed meanings, and I personally wrote a good number of them. Another good number of them were written from those that I wrote. And while I'm a stickler for accuracy, I wasn't paid to do academic research on the history of birthstones, so I took all my information from the internet. Thus, in the span of only about twenty years, we've created a new, rapidly modulating history of birthstones that's rooted only in the ether like an air plant. And nested inside these apocryphal origin stories is the arbitrary assignation of meanings to birthstones in the first place as mise en abyme of the original ascriptions of meaning to the sounds and symbols of language itself.

I participate in a laundering of language and history that's antithetical to my work as a poet wherein I try to make plain the falsities of consensual reality and to demonstrate how historical narratives are written and run away with. The internet and the language of commerce tangled within it is a widening gyre of misinformation that kills words dead. (Note that according to the internet, where the rumor first spread, it's apocryphal that Beat poet Lew Welch wrote Raid's famously redundant slogan.)

Recently I've been writing faux blog posts for a company that sells a libido-boosting mechanical product for menopausal women. I write chatty lifestyle posts under a moniker that my friend calls "Fake Kate." Fake Kate has a whole life that bears little resemblance to my own, although we share some favorite recipes and a husband who eats his cereal too loudly. At one point I was asked to incorporate quizzes, and I wrote one about menopause symptoms that contained the question, "Which of the following is *not* a symptom of menopause?" I didn't anticipate how hard it would be to find a non-menopause-related symptom. Hair-loss, tooth decay, body odor, "burning mouth," brittle nails, insomnia, dry skin, dizziness, flatulence...taking into account innumerable blogs, message boards, chatrooms, medical sites and women's magazine web features devoted to menopause, there is nary a bodily complaint that is not attributable to the cessation of menses.

As the internet folds into itself like a marble cake, its role as a catch-all for individual experience—as corrective to the consensual collective—can be read as rendering all categories of experience meaningless. Language is made of inter-nesting sets whereby we understand ourselves, but perhaps it can proliferate to a degree that undoes its fundamental role of facilitating communication, i.e., if the symptoms of menopause are just about anything, then menopause means nothing at all.

Menopause is real, though, and actually only refers to one thing— the cessation of menses.

Language is escaping us, where the verb is both active and passive—the words evading us and released like flatulence.

Adam Gordon is preoccupied with "profound experiences" of art and trying to detect whether or not someone is having one, but can't tell when he's having one himself. In one scene his deep analysis of what he believes to be the put-on profound expressions of a group of people listening to guitar music gets overtaken by the actual affecting qualities of the music. Phoniness and sincerity intercut and overwrite one another throughout the book, making it hard to tell who's real, who's fake, and most of all who's most deplorable.

Adam's genuineness detector really appears to fail him in regard to the two women he loves, who both either are or seem to be flawlessly brilliant, beautiful and unflappable. Adam can't tell a profound experience from a performance, even his own, and I can't tell if Ben Lerner is delivering actual feminine clichés or if I'm supposed to understand these idealized depictions as another blind spot in Adam's search for authenticity. And to what degree are these women performing their smooth unflappability and is this a question that Lerner wants us to ask?

Intentional fallacies fly out the window in the face of this degree of self-reflexivity. I mean, go ahead, ask me anything about what I'm trying to do, although I'm trying to make it so you won't have to.

Portrait of Ben Lerner:

*If I told him would he like it. Would he like it if I told him.*

I don't know Ben Lerner.

In *An Army of Lovers* the speakers suffer from their insufficient ability to act politically to mitigate suffering. They create sound and performance art pieces in solidarity with the prisoners at Abu Ghraib as well as in complicity with the captors. Naturally, they know these are effete gestures of privilege, and so suffer some more.

But they don't want to mitigate suffering—they would have it eradicated. Because they can't, they want to *be* suffering. Because they don't—can't—unjustly suffer in the hands of others, they have to suffer at their own hands, to suffer themselves. When gestures of art fail, they turn into themselves and their bodies, which blister, ooze and fester with leaking growths and holes.

I once saw a musical about Guantanamo written and directed by David Buuck. This preoccupation with military prisons feels like a refuge for the psychically exhausted—a dream of the trenches, of being involuntarily and unjustly subjected to harm at the hands of a corrupt system. Some dangerous things feel safe because you only have to survive them, and wrongful detention in a shitty government-run prison is the safest such thing I can think of.

Is there a subjectier subject position than political prisoner? To be pinned by interrogation light, caught behind bars—or in front of them—through which who's going to kiss your head before going to bed.

If you can't be in the trenches you can lie cold and naked next to them.

Motherhood is close. Quite close.

In *To the Lighthouse*, while pacing and staring into "the dark of human ignorance," Mr. Ramsay catches sight of his wife reading to their youngest child and finds consolation in the domestic scene that he is quick to deprecate, "as if to be caught happy in a world of misery was for an honest man the most despicable of crimes."

At the end of *An Army of Lovers*, under their noms de guerre of Koki and Demented Panda, David Buuck and Juliana Spahr semi-self-mockingly deep-breathe on yoga mats and worry that their double-donut-hole collaboration on ravaged-urban-site investigation and the book itself "…seemed so focused on the I, I, I of yet more autobiography, memoir, bourgeois individualist lyricism, and North American navel-gazing…"

By this point, Demented Panda has ditched the metonymic stroller she pushed around in the beginning, seeming to have thrown over her already all-but-absented baby for her foregone failures to make socially meaningful art. And yet, in the interim, her body is overtaken by a tick-borne sickness that induces a nipple-like protrusion she can't stop fingering, and this—this—I sympathize with.

Mrs. Ramsay worries that her children "will never be so happy again."

98

*To the Lighthouse* ends with Lily Briscoe finishing her mise-en-abyme painting that stands for the book itself by drawing a line down the middle. I have only my book and everything in it to represent my book, and my line the line between all barely- and in-distinguishable things. This line you see is vanishing.

## DREAM OF THE TRENCHES

*Once there was weather and people just lived with it. If you were plan-ning a picnic or an outdoor wedding, say, you'd have what was called a "contingency plan."*

The Eyewitnesses are laughing. We've heard this one before—doz-ens of times—but are no longer able to turn them off.

We fortress ourselves with blankets, but can't help the sound, and pull the blankets aside whenever we hear mention of class-action suits that might behoove us, rare exsanguinating illnesses, and re-markable forms of extinct life.

So we teach the children to scoff and throw things at the screen. But we don't want to break it, so replace our rougher projectiles with tissue-paper missiles we make especially for this purpose. It starts to feel like love.

*Weather caused all kinds of inconveniences. Sometimes it was so cold you could see your own breath.*

We grow tired and let the children nod in the glow, which begins to feel like weather. It spares us the uncomfortable reminder of our own exhalations, however.

## DRIVING TO MARGARET'S MOTHER'S MEMORIAL SERVICE

At the time of writing, I've been listening to the same CD in my car for almost two years. Even Willie knows it by heart.

I don't play it over and over because I love it. For a while I just listened to it because it was there and I was too tired or distracted to change it. But now I'm scared to take it out. I'm familiar with every note of every instrument and the ways they interact. I can reproduce every fillip of the singer's vibrato. For a while the songs would get stuck in my head, but I seem to have crossed a threshold where they've actually merged with my brain and don't get lodged there like foreign objects.

This sounds like an exercise in deep listening, but I think it's part of my obsessive fear of mediation—a different CD might divert or determine me. This familiar music is so simultaneously present and absent, it's as though my mind now moves in counterpoint to it. I might be dependent on it to think.

I do my best thinking at red lights, but I have the misfortune of living in a state where it's legal to turn right after stopping at them. People behind me are always honking when I don't turn right on red, which I'm pretty sure I am not obligated to do.

*3. It is absolutely essential that you continue.*

In a 2014 review Ben Lerner discusses *My Struggle*'s "radical inclu-
siveness," where the exhaustiveness of information leads to infor-
mation's exhaustion—like a fully sploozed toothpaste tube, its use-
fulness canceled by use. All events and details have equal weight,
each signifying nothing so much as the impossibility of according
any relative importance. In Lerner's own work information isn't
exhaustive, but relative importance is inverted—an act of mass ter-
ror takes a way-back seat to routine dramas of daily life. And yet
to call this an inversion is disingenuous, since it mirrors my actual
experience as a member of the sets of the safe and the fortunate.

In a meta-melodramatic move, Knausgaard's anti-fascist enact-
ment of utter mundanity borrows the title of Hitler's autobiog-
raphy. Ben Lerner does a similar thing with his evocation of the
bombing in *Leaving the Atocha Station*, only the "leaving" is a tri-
ple donut hole, suggesting a train leaving the station pre-disaster,
Adam Gordon leaving it in the aftermath, and the author all but
leaving it out of his book altogether. At both the time of writing
and of my penultimate draft (if there's even a difference), the sixth
volume of *My Struggle* has not yet appeared in English, but I gath-
er it partly concerns the 2011 Oslo summer-camp massacre.

Lerner calls *My Struggle* "radically coextensive with a life," an "ab-
ject self-exposure from which we can't look away." Nowhere in this

review does Lerner allude to his own work, which is the right thing to do, but also a joke (by which I mean "folly," but in the sense of "bananas," not "disaster"). Applying the problem or the practice or the process to itself, Knausgaard and Lerner both squint at the line between verisimilitude and authenticity, limning the reaches of the whole world and the limits of the individual operating in it. What both opposed to *An Army of Lovers* show is there's a difference between airing your festering wounds and decorating your bandages with them.

The word "praxis" annoys me. Is it the practice of practice? Meta-practice? A more active kind of practice?

Is it like "being"?

I can get behind that. By "behind" I mean something like an eclipsed thing, in syzygy, one definition of which is "any two related things, either alike or opposite."

Some celestial bodies' light is inherent, others' is reflected, and that I often can't tell the difference is where everything meets, stops, and makes further depth impossible. But what if this vanishing line is the best that you get, the suture itself, the dog hair stuck to the hole in your eye in the mirror. What if the line is the seam, the stratum where barely distinguishable things meet and press together so tightly that something precious forms and sploozes from between.

Q: What would happen if you succeeded at breaking writing?

At this late draft, I'm tempted to go back and add "meta" to my list of terms to stop using, but a thing is only useful if you use it. The best I can do is to cancel it with use, to self-consume it into a continuous absence I can live with.

A: all the things that can be said about saying in all the ways they can be said

("This" is wishful thinking.)

Q: What is the difference between "practice" and "process"?

A: acuteness and chronicity

("Being" is both a noun and a verb.)

I want to be and see the green screen.

The vents grow famous. We had thought our interest was exceptional, but the Eyewitnesses begin haunting the trenches with submersibles and so much light that we worry for the good of the dark-dwellers, even the eyeless. And the bioluminescent—what will become of their implicit radiance?

The insistent introduced light shifts our fixation to fluorescence—the borrowed wattage of coruscating fish and brittle stars in the shallower aquatic zones. Luminous jellyfish like gibbous green moons.

In all the effulgence we grow confused, like moths bumping in a sea of porch lights. In time we trade our locked-in syndrome for Stockholm, begin a slow, effervescent ascent toward the littoral.

Some light disarms its objects.

What happens when subjectivity is exhausted? I mean the smoking ant on both sides of both the cloche and the starlit magnifying glass.

You can't break writing by writing—failure enacting failure cancels into something else. But I keep my eye hole out for a kind of uncreative writing that actually uncreates itself. (How will I then write after it, though?)

> Willie: Are we there yet?
> Me: We're here!
> Willie: What?
> Me: *(singing)* Here we aaaare!
> Willie: When are we going to be there?
> Me: We can only be here, never there.
> Willie: Mommy!
> Me: *(thinking)* There, there.
> Baby: Waaah!
> Me: *(laughing)* There is no there here.
> Willie: Daddy!
> Daddy: Hey Willie, what's that coming out of those towers?
> Me: *(thinking)* Steam.
> Baby: Waaah!
> Daddy: Hot dogs?
> Willie: Steam.

In the end Adam Gordon is insupportable. His persona fails him and his relentless parsing of experience is at last overtaken by his actual experience—matter and antimatter meet, pronouns and referents collapse together like a disturbed soufflé. He becomes a black hole and falls into it.

"I have never been here, I said to myself. You have never seen me."
—Adam Gordon

A hole of more than two dimensions is a tube and this one slips through itself like a water snake toy. At the end is a skylight under which there are people who turn out to be actual, rather than mirrors and foils for Adam's obsessive self-scrutiny. There are also war and ecological disaster and other forms of the actual that Adam has been so doggedly avoiding while doing donuts inside his cloche.

Q: Are there different kinds of actual?

A: Duh.
A: Watch your language.

Q: What if this were the antecedent of "this"?

*... I've fought with all my strength...*

108

("with" meaning both "using" and "against").

I still don't know how to write anymore again.

I've written a recipe.

Ingredients:

- *My Struggle* as an act of "literary suicide"—Knausgaard
- "'Literary suicide'—a death both in and of literature." —Lerner
- "Afterlife"—a life both in and after death[1]—Me[2]

Directions:

Take one square layer cake from the freezer.

With *Leaving the Atocha Station* I was sure that Ben Lerner had done himself in. He exhausted himself in it. I don't know him, but worried about him a little bit. At the time of writing the previous sentence, his next novel had not yet come out, but by Draft Eleven I have read and resolved not to write about it, lest going back to the future render my previous thoughts anachronistic. At the time of whichever draft it is in which I'm writing this, I am ready to report that in *10:04* both author and authorial content are fully present, whether undead or at their own funerals[3]; that representation turns out to be a water snake toy whose endless involution keeps somehow revealing a new surface, like those fabric towel rolls you still sometimes see in public bathrooms.

[2] I'll never survive myself—"survive" meaning both to outlive and live *given.*

Most things have been depicted ([1]"to write after" means both "subsequent to" and "in homage").

[3] "Always," "sometimes" and "never" are each an opposite of each.

If you could talk about your cake and see it, too?

*Mmm*

looks good enough to speak.

I have a chronic preoccupation with the 1940 Tacoma Narrows Bridge collapse, as recorded on 16 mm film and viewed in my seventh-grade science class. I've tried to write about it more than once. Or when I try to write about other things its image comes at me like a close-up of a star scaled to the appearance of the field through which I'm hurtling. But I really have no business with it, since I can't understand the physics.

The bridge failure was long attributed to harmonic resonance produced by a critical wind frequency. Turns out, though, that the cause was actually "aeroelastic flutter," which sounds lovely and ethereal, like the rising motion of an animated tinsel angel, rather than a force that can take out a dependent roadbed and leave its suspension cables slack and flapping.

(There actually are degrees of actuality since everything is founded on a mystery or a set of mysteries to which there either are no answers or to which the answers are chronically unknowable or else we just don't know them.)

(Some things aren't real, but everything has something in common, if only lack of anything in common, which is a cheap paradox, but has to do with sets and my sense that they're important, even if I have no business with them either, since I can't understand the math.)

(And what happens when everything becomes parenthetical? Do your points have to nest in sets like matryoshka or can they march toward a vanishing line like railroad ties? All I know is they're looking for corners, which is the point I'm trying to get at. It's hard to turn back.)

I persist in imagining the wind and the bridge collapsing together in an angelic feat of throat singing whose self-completing overtones make a suturing bridge insupportable.

I'm preoccupied with site and my reflection in its impervious surface. I want to dig in as to a bottomless grave and make it metonymous for the world, but I feel shut out by my ignorance of physics, architecture, anthropology, sociology, religion, economics, art history, geology, music, cuisine, linguistics, animal husbandry, prehistory, and cosmology (among the other disciplines). I want to look down and have the ground funnel out in the shape of a right-side-up, but underground mountain. But on the other side of the earth is another site whose deepest layers begin and end at my feet.

I don't know how to talk about anything after Robert Smithson. How do you do after a man who died in a crash with his own artwork?

(Only a cocker spaniel died when the Tacoma Bridge gave way.)

What happens when the frame in which what you're trying to say falls away?

A vehicle hurtles into space.

I'd like to restabilize authorship, wrap myself in intention like a sweater, but all in all is all we are and forever just a cipher.

I've noticed about a lot of these meta-things-à-clef that they are easy to read in the sense that they don't use disjunctive language to describe disjunctive experience. But these books are *about* the search for a way to formally enact disjunctive experience. Maybe syntax has already been bent and broken so many times and in so many places that it's a boneless shmoo we can no longer make new. Maybe we've been making the form the content for so long that returning to narrative coherence is like coming up for air or getting sploozed out the other side or a kind of zeitgeist artisanal upcycling à la a twelve-dollar jar of farmer's market pickles. Maybe it's a screen of the sort that divides the room and which side of it you're on. Maybe it's the back of the mirror. Whatever its nature, I suspect that it's born of exhaustion.

In both *Leaving the Atocha Station* and *An Army of Lovers* the experiential disjunction is between what the speakers/characters/writers want to be able to effect with language and what they are able to. Both are about the impotence of language in a fucked-up world that needs this would-be sharpest of tools to get in there and fix it. Both are aware that sincerity and irony are flipsides of a junk nickel that buys you zip from your coin-op head.

*4. You have no other choice, you must go on.*

By "coin-op" I mean contingent, as everyone is, but you have to learn to live with it. How to push through and out the other side? In a terminal about-face, *An Army of Lovers* whips out an old-fashioned crescendo of hope for a kind of personal, active, embodied relentlessness manifested in symbiotic acts of sex and street-style protest. But this hope feels disingenuous after the authors have systematically machine-gunned down every literary *truc*, tradition, strategy, or formal possibility, culminating in the appropriation of a high-Raymond-Carver story wherein they involute their layers of cynicism to such a degree that in the end they've drawn a big black blank that wants to be an abyss, but isn't.

Following a book-long demonstration of necessary, comprehensive artistic failure at the hands of the working tool of a broken system, *An Army of Lovers* ends in a Song-of-Myselfish blab of the scab in which "what comes out of you or me comes out of all of us," but only because you have to say it that way anymore or be waved aside for utter interiority. The book's failure is manifold—it disingenuously positions itself as a complete failure by definition, and then tacks on an abstract rallying cry that fails both in its cursoriness and its contamination of the complete failure the book promised to deliver.

I want to hate *Leaving the Atocha Station*, but it matches the *trompe l'oeil* eyelid-motif wallpaper lining my eyelids, which cocoons me as it curls in from the edges. All of Adam Gordon's hash-smoking is boring, but it does evoke the capsule containing my brain on this breathless, seemingly endless drive to a funeral on the Cape.

I am also preoccupied by Stanley Milgram's 1962 Obedience Experiment, as recorded on black-and-white film and viewed in the Holocaust unit of my eighth-grade social studies class. Following the trial of Nazi war criminal Adolf Eichmann, Milgram was studying the lengths to which people will go in obedience to authority. Test subjects, or "teachers," were instructed to administer electric shocks to "learners," who, unbeknownst to the teachers, were paid actors. Every time learners furnished incorrect answers to what was said to be a memory test, the teachers would deliver what they believed were real shocks of incrementally higher voltage, the last of which would be fatal, if actual.

The actors would scream, moan, pound on the wall and, finally, fall silent as the most severe shock was administered. Teachers would shake, sweat and beg to stop, but whenever they faltered, Milgram would urge them to continue with a series of four impassive verbal prods.

65% of teachers administered the final, would-be-fatal shock. Over time, variations on the experiment were performed in many different countries, with no appreciable difference in results.

At the time of my final revision, Volume Six of *My Struggle* has still not appeared in English. Supposedly it also explains Knausgaard's cooptation of Hitler, but I'm beginning to think I don't need to read it.

Let this remain a lain abyss. I'm exhausted/consumed/canceled/finished.

The site that Juliana Spahr and David Buuck and their characters choose to obsess over in the mise-en-abyme art project that is one meta- removed from the meta-meta project that is *An Army of Lovers* itself is simultaneously un-self-conscious and extremely so. The site contains both a lot of ugly urban detritus and a pair of sculptures denoting HERE and THERE on either side of the line dividing Berkeley and Oakland. (Or is the "there" on the Berkeley side? Which would Stein hate more?) Their project, they say, is to explore "how a site can be a complex cipher of the unstable relationships that define the present crises and their living within them."

Cladding irony in sincerity together with the inverse is a conceptualist cul-de-sac, a closed system that might feel like having your words and eating them, but is more of a lunch combo with John Corbett.

Working against a system with its working tool doesn't work. You have to get outside, and yet there's no way out but through. So, what do you do? All I know is my urgent need to get to the bottom of just one thing—this one leaf on this here tree—so I can seal my preoccupation, its praxis and the process into a capsule and launch it.

*Sayonara*, space lady. I hope this proves what you crash into.

## DREAM OF THE TRENCHES

Between the glittering pelagic and the cut-off depths of the trenches life relies on marine snow. Necrotic bits and bacteria from the teeming light-filled layers above slowly fall and nourish the inhabitants of this place between surfaces.

We can't fathom having no horizon. At night we look up and marvel at the space between stars—millions of light-years we can pinch between our fingers. This act of possession gives us hope that the children might find a way to survive there. Whether this would constitute compromise or capitulation we are not certain.

Fluorescing in the flicker from the screen, we incline our heads and catch its rotten confetti on our tongues.

Whether we have walked in an actual field is neither here nor there. What's here is a dusting of digestible flakes backlit on the meniscus of the nearing surface, our gaping lips, the glowing projection we can see our heads in.

## DRIVING TO MARGARET'S MOTHER'S MEMORIAL SERVICE

The opposite of a profound experience of art might be church. Still, I choke through the hymns over which the choir sings a descant, our voices raised in unison, filling the dome, limning the meniscus.

Are individual and collective experience one another's donut holes?

During a recent sermon about man as nature's mirror—nature's means of apprehending itself—I was thinking, what happens then when man checks itself out in a puddle? The mirrors crash like cymbals and fall to pieces. They might look like bits of broken sky, but each intact fragment contains the whole blue dome.

There's no way out but through.

It's imprudent to point out others' more successful attempts at what you're trying to do (unless pointing them all out is your point...), but I have to mention *Horton Hears a Who*. I have no idea what Willie gets from it, since he's still tucked inside his cloche without any sense of its presence, but this is one of his favorite books and it always gives me the chills when the Whos yell:

> We are here
> We are here
> We are here

Think of picture postcards swirling down the Arno.

Think of flash-mob mall *Messiah* videos on YouTube.

Think again.

How to write after Dr. Seuss.

## DREAM OF THE TRENCHES

At last there is only light. Without any shadows it is difficult to see and our eyes fuzz over like milk glass. Our remaining vision consists of glints and flashes. We rely on the Eyewitnesses who assure us there's nothing to see here. We move on.

We keep our faces inclined toward the screen. The still discernible flicker of the children's faces fills us—their intellects will not want for anything in this exhaustive world.

Even a fish will not survive the sea. Here on the surface it is bright—scintillating, really—and getting brighter by the minute. We emerge from dissipating dreams of the vents. Our cataracts contain us.

According to the internet, the face of Resusci Annie, the ubiqui-tous CPR training doll, is that of a young woman who drowned in the Seine in the 1880s. Her death mask was cast in plaster, dubbed *l'Inconnue*, and sold widely as decorative wall art. The Norwegian toymaker who created Annie in the 1950s remembered the beatific mask that hung in his grandparents' living room and thought it suited the purpose of his dummy.

The identity of the real girl and whether she threw herself or fell into the river remain unknown, as does the degree to which any of these things matter [I want to say "in the grand scheme of things," but I think that's the opposite of what I mean. (But what's the difference between mattering and meaning?)].

The girl and her image are sutured to my sense that identity is lapidary, formed by a crushing pressure and a careful carving, both the highest form of decoration and hard enough to perform feats of incision. (You can tell it's real if it scratches the mirror.)

Nothing is what it actually seems.

Your head is a hall of screens.

The flat light falls like snow into ready-made men flapping it into angel impressions. But against its glare, its white noise, its glowing green, I suddenly think I can think. Perhaps it's that I can make out the glass and which side of it I'm on matters less than the fact of it.

It's hard to see the real abysses in white-out conditions, but if you stack up enough of the laid ones sometimes they'll fool you.

(By "you" I mean "me.")

(This fatuous use of pronouns is the opposite of John Ashbery.)

The subtitle of Stein's poem "If I Told Him" is "A Completed Portrait of Picasso," which creates a triple-thought non-non-dissonance since completion is antithetical to it and her whole mode of apprehending apprehension. But her loupe is a loop and they're both strange, so like a donut containing both of its holes, the highest order of complete.

*Let me recite what history teaches. History teaches.*

We agree to agree—

*I have never been here. You have never seen me.*

—as far from the world as agreeing with it.

The Bourne Bridge sutures the mainland to the Cape, where sea roses grow in the shape of their resistance to the wind off the sea at the center of their name. Their dirt-sweet scent merges with the smell of the nameless pavement equivalent of petrichor.

I could title this mess *The Problem with Portraiture*, remove the content from its frame, hang one or the other on the wall and walk away. But such still life would be disingenuous when I can't stop blinking, thinking to myself that this is all there is outside of its exigencies, without which I'd pinch out like a pointless star.

(Kate excises the redundancy "thinking to myself" from Draft Five but by Draft Thirteen says I've earned it. I pat myself on the back and now how to write after it.)

My exhaustion is reflected in a three-way mirror, where the seamstress is trying to pin me—

*Would he like it if Napoleon if Napoleon if I told him.*

("Napoleon" meaning *millefeuille.*)

"Seamstress" meaning OED.

Are there other names for particular smells?

How to write after Pachelbel.

*DRIVING TO MARGARET'S MOTHER'S MEMORIAL SERVICE*

I pretty often think about Thoreau and what it means to live deliberately. If I were to leave my family, my comfortable life, the dog, lock myself in a cellar or aerie, what would I need to be doing or thinking to exist completely and on purpose? What is the difference between living deliberately and at capacity? Do I keep my eye to the grindstone or the furthest reaches of the unknown or the putting-on of shoes in the middle? I have an unfortunate sense that, for me, purpose has come to mean being glued to my computer.

If I could make complete sense of every word, I'd be golden. But instead, I'm dressed in black, on a steam-bath of a day in July, driving to a funeral for someone I hardly knew. (I long ago lost the arc of this trip to the Cape that I took nearly six years ago at publication date. The conceit has failed to fold into the cake.)

When writing a biography—whether auto-, fake, fictional or actual—you have to choose which facts to include. A practiced writer will slip in interesting details and seeming coincidences and leave it to the reader to decide if they're relevant or telling or red herrings or not. You know how when you learn a new word you start hearing it all the time? It's not that you didn't hear it before, it's just that you began noticing yourself hearing it. What constitutes a pattern and how do you tell the start of it from a part of it?

There's no such thing as a coincidence *or* a red herring (which are either opposites or nearly the same), unless you believe in ciphers. (A cipher can be a secret or nonentity and at the time of writing this ending I no longer know which I meant or mean.)

I am sorry to say that John Ashbery has just died.

I have a desperate sense of wanting to keep Ben Lerner alive just so that he might attend his anachronistic funeral.

I'm too exhausted to tie them up so I'm making a list:

<u>Loose Ends</u>
Jack Kerouac
James Joyce
Christmas?

Is that all?

I read *On the Road* just after driving from Massachusetts to San Francisco the day after graduating from college. (I was going to spend the summer waiting tables, but stayed for eleven years.) Despite my English degree, I've never read *Finnegan's Wake* or *Ulysses*. I read *Portrait of the Artist as a Young Man* more than once, though, and umpteen times "The Dead," which is a long and boring account of a Christmas party all over which snow falls, suggesting both time immemorial and immanence.

"Ove" is pronounced "OO-vah."

(One last Q: is it okay that *Q* and *A* have fallen away?)

David Buuck and Juliana Spahr are actual exceptional poets.

Neither have I read *The Golden Notebook*.

## DRIVING TO MARGARET'S MOTHER'S MEMORIAL SERVICE

Perhaps it ends not with disintegration or collapse, but another twist in the longest distance.

How many drafts were there of *Leaves of Grass*? Whitman kept changing the frontispiece to reflect the modulation of his aspect. At last he looks like Santa and how to be after that?

A motif of *10:04* is the family photo in *Back to the Future* from which Marty fades as he messes with his parents' past.

"To be in any form, what is that?"—*Song of Myself*

There's no such thing as half a hole, even if only half is sutured.

Forms become inadequate for the things that they have shown us.

*DRIVING TO MARGARET'S MOTHER'S MEMORIAL SERVICE*

Some dangerous things feel safe because you only have to survive them, but what if the greatest danger is of completion? What would happen if I found the exact language to describe my experience?

I just hope that the set of all sets really is a member of itself.

Can you experience yourself without thinking of it? If not, then you're cursed to mediation, both active and passive, nature and mirror, and this

        this

        this ("that

last Onset"?) is actually all there is.

How to write after this? How to slip out the other side? Where and what is the skylight?

        Black twinkle-shaped bits of night
        fall to the paper, the screen, look
        like letters. The meniscus admits
        light in the shape of its perforations.

Before going to bed each night I check on the kids. I crouch and kiss the baby through the bars of the crib, in tears I cannot see to see.

"It seemed to her such nonsense—inventing differences"—Mrs. Ramsay

We call the baby Maggie.

In the end, Adam Gordon is the same as himself.

Is this a fillip of hope for unmediated experience? No. I think it's for the possibility of exhaustion, of exhausting your subjectivity, at least momentarily. Adam's efforts to locate a profound experience of art and a pure form of poetry are founded in a fear of "the triumph of the actual." In the end the actual does triumph, but turns out to be full of real abysses rather than the laid ones he was looking for. In his crushing self-compaction something sploozes out and while I'm not sure of its nature, it feels like something else.

> To have my words and eat them,
> to write myself into the corner,
> to screw everything down until
> that's what I'm driving for.

> Whether we begin and end in a place
> more woods or hole I can't say

> and the problem with if you unfolded forever
> is forever's how long it would make.

## TRAVEL PROHIBITED IN BREAKDOWN LANE

If, in our exhaustive world, all writing feels fake and duplicitous, what's left but to turn into words, as I might into the guardrail?

"Saturation" and "exhaustion" can be opposites, but in this case they're the same and between them contain what I hope is something approaching "this."

But between the self and its reflection there's a blinking lid.

## SOME WORKS

*1984*, George Orwell, 1949

*A Room with a View*, E.M. Forster, 1908

*An Army of Lovers*, David Buuck & Juliana Spahr, 2013

*Angle of Yaw*, Ben Lerner, 2006

*John Ashbery: Collected Poems, 1956-1987* (Library of America, No. 187), 2008

"Each Cornflake," *London Review of Books*, Ben Lerner, 2014

"Elena Ferrante on the Origins of her Neapolitan Novels," Megan O'Grady, *Vogue*, 2014

*The Golden Notebook*, Doris Lessing, 1962

*The Great Gatsby*, F. Scott Fitzgerald, 1925

*Horton Hears a Who*, Dr. Seuss, 1952

"I Heard a Fly Buzz..," Emily Dickinson, 1896

"If I Told Him: A Completed Portrait of Picasso," Gertrude Stein, 1924

*The Journalist*, Harry Mathews, 1994

*Leaves of Grass*, Walt Whitman, 1855

*Leaving the Atocha Station*, Ben Lerner, 2011

*My Struggle*, Karl Ove Knausgaard, 2013–2018

*Pamela: A Novel*, Pamela Lu, 1998

*To the Lighthouse*, Virginia Woolf, 1927

*Where Angels Fear to Tread*, E.M. Forster, 1905

*Zelda*, Nancy Milford, 1970

*SLOW STRUCTURES*

## THE LESSON

I miss that warble-y fake pathos from the '80s, à la Ric
Ocasek. We will never be the same. Our pathos is real, but
turned inside-out so as only to appear that way. When I
was in seventh grade I had a science teacher called Mrs.
Harris. She collected road kill and kept it in the class-
room freezer for use during animal anatomy lessons. One
time she pulled out a fresh raccoon, stuck her hand in
its ripped abdomen, flipped its skin inside-out and wag-
gled its leg. The classroom duly exploded in screams and
groans. I remember noticing how much she enjoyed her
performance. One time there was a weekend-long power
outage and all of Mrs. Harris's specimens defrosted. On
Monday morning the school reeked and the classroom
was cordoned off, but I must have gotten in somehow be-
cause I know that this was the first time I saw maggots.

## NATURE

Emerson was only the first American to join the continuum of longing for unmediated, extemporary connection to the world. I mean with time to talk about it. I feel most fully realized not when I'm connecting, though, but bristling with pure yearning, my million filaments reaching and waving like a fiber-optic Medusa or anemone. Words will always get in the way—you can't be a transparent eyeball and see it, too. I often think of Emerson on cool fall days when the air and light are so clear you can almost hear them, like the ringing sound of a finger running around the thinnest crystal rim. Listen: what I mean to say is something about procedural constraint. I build the thinnest ornament around me and reach out toward it. If you can see me inside this transparent ball, well, it only goes one way—you're just looking in the mirror.

## CAROTID ARTERY

Have you noticed that men enjoy uttering the words "ca-
rotid artery," usually accompanied by a slicing gesture at
the throat? I thought this was due to the word's sugges-
tions of violence and death. I have since realized it might
be more for the pleasure of the perfect iambic tetrameter.
So, why don't I recall ever hearing a woman say "carotid
artery"? Do I just not notice? Evidently, there was a form
of ancient Greek poetry called iambus that rendered in-
sulting language in iambic tetrameter. I want to conclude
there must be something mythopoetically manly about
this meter, but scholars have partly located the origins of
iambus in the cult of fertility goddess Demeter. Perhaps
something more essential can be drawn from the fact
that many of our most vulnerable body parts have po-
etic compound names—"Achilles tendon" (iambs), "solar
plexus" (trochees). "Fuck you," "shut up" and "buzz off" are
spondees.

## GREEN FLASH

When I was young I loved catching, no, standing on the threshold between states, say when the streetlights stuttered on at twilight. I would try to see the stick-numbers rearrange on the digital clock. What I really wanted to see, though, was the green flash that is said to sometimes spread across the sky at the exact moment of sunset over the ocean. I gazed at the horizon until it became painful. Research reveals disagreement about whether or not this is even a real phenomenon. Either way, to see it would apotheosize the threshold, although I am equally rewarded with this triangular or tripartite space between real and not-real and the unknown. What if there isn't even an answer? Here I am, stuck in a staring contest with the void while over there my kid's lower lip is twisted, trembling with potential energy. Just don't wake me when it's over.

## SACRIFICE

Once I took a proofreading test at a job interview and
only missed a non-capped "Velcro." I got the job, copy-
editing a consumer product catalog, but was never quite
right with Onesies and Thermoses. It was my role to ren-
der them "baby bodysuits" and "beverage containers" but
I felt like a traitor to the lexicon. When a brand name
slides into public usage it's called "genericide." Companies
attempt to prevent it by suggesting other generic names,
but who's ever called a trampoline a "rebound tumbler"?
Failure rarely has a stable referent. A standard feature of
Mesoamerican cities is a ball court, but anthropologists
can only guess at the rules and object of the game. One
theory says it may have been the game's winners who were
sacrificed in order to fight evil in the underworld. But
how seemingly senseless to knock off your best players,
winnow your team into impotence.

Ice seems so manual, mechanical, last century. Remember *The Mosquito Coast* and Harrison Ford dragging blocks of ice into the jungle, like some poor-man's Fitzcarraldo? It had melted by the time he got there. In Gloucester, Massachusetts the ice manufacturer that supplies the famous fishing industry is in trouble, since the ocean has been systematically strained of fish and the local fleet is dying. The other night at dinner my friend Joanna was worrying about CAPTCHAs and how they are being improved upon in a way that over time will teach the computers trying to determine whether or not we are human how to behave more like humans. She is concerned about the increasing intelligence of robots, but in a way that's too smart for me to comprehend. Meanwhile, the now-famous Gloucester ice company survives largely by selling its t-shirts, which were once featured in a movie starring George Clooney.

## THE ITCH

When I can't fall asleep at night first I count backwards from one thousand, and then I try to figure out why I am awake when the body most often possesses the means of its own mitigation—you rub spit on a mosquito bite, step on your stubbed toe, feel metaphoric, e.g., "make the most of every moment" (your life is not a bag and the capacity of time is always the same). We are so pleasingly self-contained, like one of those triangular single-slice pizza boxes you see at the airport. Of course, once it's emptied and thrown away it looks like a head, homesick for its all-but-self-same contents. Did you read that story in *The New Yorker* about the woman whose unrelentingly itchy scalp caused her to scratch right through her cranium? The itch was imaginary, but what's the difference? She scratched all the way through to her brain.

*VESSEL*

I am prepossessed with essence, which is just the kind of thing it's just like me to say. Most manmade things are defined by their functions, but what if they never get to perform them? Is a boat still a boat if it never holds a person or floats or both? What if it's unmanned, but remote-controlled, like a drone; or a Flying Dutchman, home only to ghosts; or host only to rats and corpses, save a single dormant vampire? Surely there's never been a better vessel and vehicle for horror than Klaus Kinski. And if your essential function's aesthetic, your qualitative and quantitative values are the same. Most things can be assessed relatively, but have you ever seen a bad doorway? I suppose a wall is a bad doorway, but only if you're a stickler for intentional fallacy. Either way, we are always only our ghosts to give up.

## TOO LATE

When I was in 8th grade I went on a ski trip to Vermont. I remember one evening entering a dark room and finding the members of my Unitarian youth group sprawled on beds and around the floor, silently listening to *Desperado*. We had been learning about world religions, had it intimated to us that they were all right and wrong at once—except for our own, of course, which wasn't a religion, although loosely based in the ideas of a bunch of people best known for never getting anywhere and talking about it. *Your prison is walking...*, etc. I joined my compatriots in the dark and we sort of radiated toward one another while at the same time palpating our own interior walls, like mimes. I think of this every time it rains so hard the storm drains bubble over and puke up dead leaves all over the street.

It is always a delight to use a thing for something other than its intended purpose, thus cheating the whole nomenclature system. Beauty regimens are especially conducive to product experimentation, such as dabbing hemorrhoid cream on your eye bags, or that horse shampoo girls used in high school. As a house fly tries to get outside by repeatedly throwing itself at the window, I wonder whether a name is best suited to what one wants, gets, or is designed for. When I look in the mirror I see my face fading into a modulating self whose name remains the same, as though birth were a benchmark. It might be that humans' *raison d'etre* is to apprehend ourselves getting older. How old do you have to be to say, "I was once a great beauty" and not be thought vain? Beauty is either just a fact or only the appearance of it.

## MEMORY

I can't remember a time before I had enough words to remember with, and I often wonder if my inability to remember early childhood is a memory in, just not of, itself. And are there physical differences between the things I can't remember, i.e., are some memories simply never triggered while others are inaccessible or pinched-out all together? One time my now-husband and I drove from San Francisco to the Salton Sea, which was formed in 1905 when heavy rainfall and snowmelt broke through irrigation dikes and filled an ancient dry lakebed in the desert. There were once some '50s-era resorts along the edge, but now only a few stringy encampments are left. Due to changes in the climate and agricultural water management, the sea's shoreline is rapidly receding and the salinity rising, so that, the day I was there, there was a ring of little dead fish around it.

In middle-school French class we had to choose names for ourselves. One boy went by Jacques and every time the teacher called his name, he said "strap" under his breath and we'd laugh. Mine was Catherine, which I had always wished was my given name, even though it means "innocent," which doesn't really suit me. I think of "epithet" as a prejudicial catch-all term, but it can also describe a person's actual qualities, like Catherine the Great, who was what's now known as an "enlightened despot." It's a common misconception that Rasputin was a nickname for the Romanovs' so-called "Mad Monk," since it means something along the lines of, "having strayed from the path" in Russian, but it was, in fact, the man's family name. He does appear to have been mad, though. Meanwhile, I've been called "Kate the Great" by various people my whole life, simply because it rhymes.

## SENESCENCE

You can't die of old age, but you can and likely will die
of senescence, or "aging." In other words, you will die of
a gerund, both active and hypothetical. Congratulations!
You are not a lobster. The thing about lobsters being im-
mortal is untrue, actually—they eventually grow tired and
get stuck in their incommodious exoskeletons. Just think
how comforting it would be to contain oneself to that de-
gree. They say crab meat retains the flavor of what it eats,
for which reason they're fed mangoes in the Caribbean,
per my friend Ann. But while coconut crabs are said to
taste of their name, coconuts are only a small component
of their diet. So, which follows what—the nutriment, the
flavor or the moniker? I read there's compelling evidence
that Amelia Earhart was eaten by coconut crabs. They
found fragments of a skeleton matching her description.
She was only forty.

## VICTORY

When I was eight I cut off a third of my right index finger by shutting it in the door of my parents' Ford. I remember standing in the driveway with my hand against the car, stock still and hesitating to scream because I didn't want anyone to come open the door and let my finger fall out. I think it was Michelangelo who talked about releasing the man from the marble, although I might have read that in *The Agony and the Ecstasy*, which is an incomparably cheesy novel. In any case, I was severed that day from the fact of my shape and rendered over again in veiny gray stone. They sewed my finger back on but it's always felt like the wrong one, a victorious foam extremity stabbing from the neck of *Winged Victory*. There was a crowd around her at the Louvre, or was that *Venus*?

## THE AGENT

My grandmother used to call me "Mata Hari" during my teenage dangly earrings phase and "Typhoid Mary" when I was sick. The latter is especially inaccurate, since Typhoid Mary never contracted the disease with which she infected more than fifty people. I wonder if poisonous beings are susceptible to their own poison. For instance, what would happen if one rattlesnake bit another? Of course, anti-venom is derived from the venom itself, resulting in a theoretical case of either Ouroboros or self-annihilation. If I have a defensive weapon it's words, which I use to infect myself with whatever is already eating me. The act of infection is the antidote, but it always turns out I'm impervious to both: "asymptomatic" and "asymptote" (the latter being a straight line continually approaching but never meeting a curve) come from Greek for "not falling together." Coincidentally, Mata Hari was executed for being a double agent.

One time I was asked to contribute a song to a mixed CD for a pregnant friend. The idea was for her to listen to it while giving birth. I suggested *I Wanna Be Sedated* because I always make a joke, but only later considered that a person would have to be born to it. It's a weighty onus, really, since so much music chews its feelings for you and then wings them your way on a shatter-proof plate. It seems like in addition to a meal, Death Row inmates should get to pick a last song to die to. What pre-fab feeling would you choose? When listening to the radio while driving I wonder what song might happen to be playing were I to die in a fiery car crash. All I know is I have what feels like a telling shudder every time I hear Electric Light Orchestra.

## SURVIVOR

One loves stories of the body rendered strictly functional, reduced to survival, enslaved to circumstance and its own exigencies, like that Stephen King story about the marooned surgeon who removes his limbs one by one and then eats them. Howard Blackburn was a nineteenth-century fisherman. Once during a winter storm his dory was lost at sea. The dorymate soon died, but Blackburn pushed forth, letting his mittenless fingers freeze curled around the oars. Several days later he landed on the coast of Newfoundland and was fine, although he lost all of his fingers. I want there to be a lesson in here about trimming fat, but what could be less fatty to a primate than fingers? When I was a ballet dancer my favorite step name was *fondue*, both for its onomatopoeic fluidity and evocation of cheese, which I forsook back then in the interest of a purely aesthetic thinness.

## MOTION

I love to travel, but not alone. Once on a break from school in Paris I took a train to Budapest with three friends. We slept in the great hall of a Magyar fortress, which had been converted to a bunk room. Its tall stone walls were dimly lit with sconces and lined with two-dozen-odd beds, but we were the only ones there. We each spent our days alone, supposedly exploring the city, but I just wandered around stupidly until we met for dinner and I was relieved of my own company. All day I felt tinny and hollow, like a molded chocolate figurine wrapped in thin foil. Now that I'm no longer free to go anywhere, though, I need a lot of time alone to curl into the furniture, always remembering: any reference frame that's in uniform motion with respect to an inertial frame is also an inertial frame.

## THE END


Entropy bothers me. Not the fact of it, but how it's characterized as increasing over time. It's the most counterintuitive thing I can think of. Shouldn't the concept of gradual heat death—the complete petering-out of the universe—be a thing that's described as *decreasing*? There are probably physical reasons for this cognitive glitch, and while it's not the word's fault but the directionality ascribed to its meaning, it would be nice if the word for entropy were somehow ass-backwards, too. What's worse, though, is how entropy increases into the redundant "Absolute Zero," which denotes both utter temperature and the end of it. Wouldn't "Sort-of Zero" be better? Language isn't arbitrary, but relative—the right words for the world might make sense of it. If I could be a theoretical poet and both break and make everything just by saying it, I'd be beholden only to controvertible qualities of poetry.

## CHECKPOINT

When driving Highway 1 down the center of Mexico's Baja peninsula you occasionally get stopped at military checkpoints. Uniformed men with conspicuous heavy-duty weapons press you with questions and search your car. Once in the remotest part of the central desert a soldier asked us to give him a ride somewhere. We made excuses in wild gestures and bad Spanish and during this exchange I remember being so terrified that I could feel my lungs not breathing. What I don't remember is if we gave the man and his loaded rifle a ride or not. It seems to me that the memory privileges feeling over fact. I recall so well that sustained electric-shock feeling of first love but not for whom I felt it. Or you know those mirror boxes they use to treat amputees with phantom limb pain? I see my mind that way, but without hope for alleviation.

## ACKNOWLEDGMENTS

Thank you to the editors of *Eleven Eleven*, *The Rumpus*, *Verse*, and the Essay Press digital chapbook series, who first published portions of this work.

Thank you to Mary-Kim Arnold, Joanna Howard, Lynn Melnick, Patrick Reidy, and Todd Shalom for various forms of attention to this book. Thank you to Al Filreis, whose legendary ModPo MOOC pushed this work forward and led to a valuable friendship. Thank you to Emily Alex, Sarah Gzemski, Steve Halle, and Noemi Press for the work it took to put this book into the world. Thank you to Darcie Dennigan and Kate Schapira for their faith, commiseration and expert editing; to Rusty Kinnicutt for the love and patience; and to Willie for being his best Willie, no matter what.

I will be forever indebted to Emily Cunha, Ann Huyck, and Caitlin Porter, without whose sympathy, advice, carpools, determination, and mutual exhaustion this book would not exist.

I dedicate this book to Margaret Funkhouser and to my own beloved Margaret, both from whom I've learned much.